ADV

SPECIAL 2026

Adventures, Special Edition 2026
First edition

Published by ADV/OffBeat Publishing, LLC
ISBN (Print): 978-1-950464-87-6
ISBN (ebook): 978-1-950464-91-3

CONTENTS

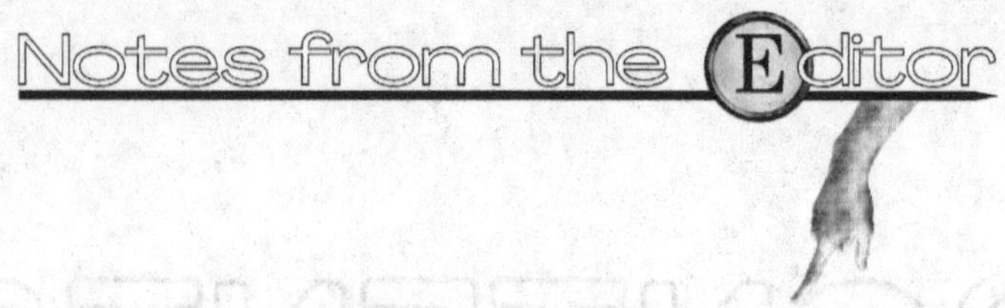

Welcome to a special edition of Adventures!

USUALLY WE LIKE TO SET OUR SIGHTS ON NOSTALGIC STORIES LARGELY FORgotten by time, but we recently have received so many good stories by current authors that we decided to create a special edition to showcase a few of them.

The stories in this edition are along the lines of what you've come to expect from us—pulp fiction essentially—so we're sure you're going to enjoy reading these stories and perhaps find a new favorite author in the process.

In this edition we have *Circus of Fear* (*A Mr. Risk Adventure*) by Evan Purcell (who recently was featured for the first time in ADV), *Mirrors* by Dale Alexander, *Paradise Lite* by Darryle Purcell, *In the Mind of the Beholder* by Murray Eiland, and three author-selected episodes from *The Intergalactic Misadventures of Henry Trevalu* from E.J. LeRoy.

After reading these original stories, we'd love to hear from you about which ones you like best, so don't be shy about emailing us. By the way, our spring issue of ADV is right around the corner, so keep an eye out for that as well.

Thanks for reading this special issue. Enjoy!

Michael Brian

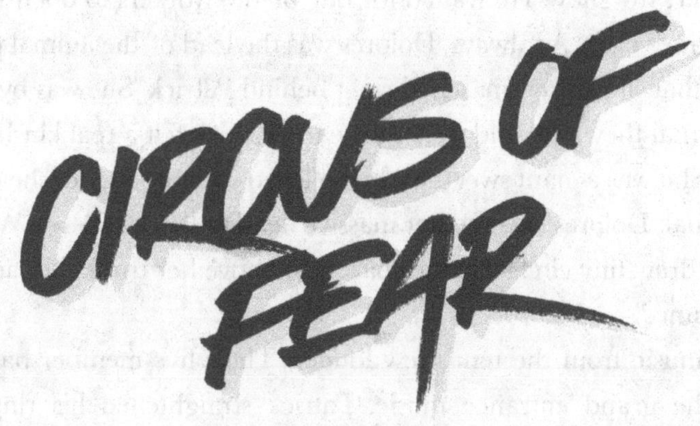

A Mr. Risk Adventure
By Evan Purcell

Patrick Garvey stood in front of the animal cages, watching as his employees rushed around to check the locks before tonight's show. The rain was getting worse by the second, with thick, cold drops plunking onto the ankle-deep mud.

Patrick considered going back inside the ring to dry off before he had to perform. After all, his men had everything under control. They knew which ropes to tie and which cages to move. Most of them had been with him since he and his family started Garvey Circus nearly ten years before. He trusted they wouldn't let him down.

But then again, Patrick also heard the grumbling, the whispers among his staff. These men (all of them burly and bearded, and most of them veterans) were thinking of leaving the circus. The recent spate of accidents had gotten them spooked, and Patrick didn't blame them. Two deaths in such a short time… that's more than just a coincidence. He had to do everything he could to prove to his men that they were safe here, that he would watch out for them. And if that meant standing out in the pouring rain, then that was what he had to do.

A trumpet blasted from the circus tents, signaling Patrick that it was time to start the show. He waited for one of the workers to open Dolores the elephant's cage. As always, Dolores was the lead of the animal parade, meaning that she always marched right behind Patrick. She was by far the oldest animal they had, and over the years, Patrick felt a real kinship with Dolores. She was a giant sweetheart who loved walnuts and forehead rubs.

As usual, Dolores lowered her massive head to Patrick's level. With one finger, he drew tiny circles on the space just above her trunk. "Ready, girl? It's showtime."

The music from the tent grew louder. Their five-member band was playing the grand entrance music. Patrick straightened his ringleader cap and started to march. Behind him, a procession of animals and their trainers followed.

When they crossed into the tent, the audience instantly burst into cheers. Even though the animals were all dripping wet from the rain, they were still beautiful, formidable creatures. With music playing and the scent of popcorn filling the air, Patrick began his march toward the center of the ring. He waved at the crowd, but his eyes were focused on the edge of the stage. He saw his sister Rebecca standing near the clowns. He wasn't surprised to see his sister there. That was her usual spot. What surprised him was the look of abject horror on her face.

Unfortunately for Patrick, that terrified expression was the last thing he would ever see. The roar of the crowd instantly went silent, and then everything went dark.

One second, Patrick was basking in applause and waiting to start the show. And the next, he was crushed under Dolores' massive feet. She'd trampled him so fast that he didn't feel a thing.

Mr. Risk sat in his study, surrounded by walls covered with antlers and shelves filled with the rarest and most ancient books. He had everything he needed for another case, everything except a client. It had been a week since he'd helped the local police catch that diamond thief. Ever since then, he and his assistant Abdul had been waiting in the house with nothing to do.

Outside, the rain was getting worse, crashing against the windows and nearly breaking the shutters. It was a terrible storm, almost as bad as the one yesterday or the day before.

This weather left Mr. Risk seriously depressed, not because of the rain itself, but because it kept all the criminals cooped up inside. If the day was sunny and breezy, there would probably be a few more bank robbers or car thieves out there, and then Mr. Risk would finally have something to do.

Silent as always, Abdul walked into the room. He was carrying a platter of hors d'oeuvres on a silver tray. He had pickled figs and miniature sandwiches and even a little blood pudding.

"What's all this?" Mr. Risk was surprised by the amount of food. They'd already shared a dinner of sauteed tilapia in bourbon sauce.

"We are expecting guests, master," Abdul answered solemnly.

Mr. Risk raised an eyebrow. Abdul hadn't told him about any visitors today. One of his assistant's many jobs was to schedule appointments. He'd been doing it for years, and he'd never forgotten to tell his boss beforehand. "And who is coming?"

Abdul shrugged his massive shoulders.

"You don't know?"

"You said our dry spell wouldn't last more than a week. I trust your promise. The last client was seven days ago, so… Tonight, we have a new client."

Mr. Risk smiled. He glanced once more at the snack tray and realized that the foods were all Abdul's favorites. Clearly, Abdul had done this intentionally. If no one came, then he'd get to eat it all himself. Very clever. "Well, in case no one shows up, help yourself."

At that, Abdul grabbed a pickled fig and popped it into his mouth. As he swallowed, a loud, frantic knock bashed against the door. Someone was outside.

Abdul raced to the door and opened it. A stunningly beautiful blonde woman stood at the doorstep with a wall of rain as her backdrop. A small, pink purse hung off her shoulder. Even though she was drenched, she looked like she'd stepped right off a movie screen.

The woman nervously looked into Abdul's dark eyes. "Are you… Mr. Risk?"

The real Mr. Risk stepped forward. "Why yes. *I* am. Come in."

Abdul closed the door. The woman wiped wet strands of hair from her face, but she didn't walk any closer. Abdul gestured for her to come into the room, but she chose to linger by the front door.

"My name is Rebecca Garvey," she said, "and I need your help."

Mr. Risk, who had stood as soon as the woman walked into the room, began to pace across the carpet. He was scanning through his memory, trying to think of why that last name sounded so familiar. Garvey. He'd seen it recently, written on a poster for… something. He couldn't remember.

"Garvey?" Abdul asked. "From Garvey Circus?"

And just like that, Mr. Risk remembered where he'd seen the name. Garvey Circus was one of those traveling shows that pulls up a tent for a couple days and then moves on. He'd seen the flyers all around town.

The woman nodded. "That's my family's circus. Have you been?"

Abdul didn't answer.

Mr. Risk, of course, had never bothered to go to the circus. He didn't understand the appeal of watching people walk on tightropes and stick their head in a lion's mouth. As a man who didn't know fear, the spectacle of the circus simply wasn't that exciting.

Rebecca remained by the entrance. When it was obvious that she wasn't going to come any closer, Mr. Risk told his assistant, "Maybe Miss Garvey is interested in an hors d'oeuvre to soothe her nerves."

Abdul brought her the silver tray of snack food. She took one look at it and said, "Actually, do you have water? I know I'm already soaking wet, but my throat is a little dry. From all the screaming."

Abdul disappeared into the other room, carrying the tray with him. Mr. Risk assumed his servant would polish off the rest of the food when no one was looking.

"Miss Garvey, tell me why you're here."

"I'm worried about my safety," Rebecca said. "And I'm worried that we'll have to close down our circus."

"Why?" Mr. Risk asked. "Aren't you the 'first festival for fun, fear, and frivolity'?" He was quoting their flyer. "Why would you close?"

Lightning flashed in the window behind Rebecca, making her jump. She crossed her arms over her chest. She looked seconds away from losing her courage and racing out of the house. Mr. Risk considered walking to her, comforting her, but he knew that with clients like her, it was always better to wait for them to come to him.

When she didn't say anything, Mr. Risk asked his question again: "Why would you close?"

"Because of the gypsy curse!" she blurted out. Then she covered her mouth, as if she'd accidentally screamed some horrible swear word. She forced herself to calm down and continued, "I know it sounds crazy. Up until recently, I never imagined that I'd actually believe in something so… ludicrous."

"A gypsy curse," Mr. Risk repeated. "And what are the effects of this curse?"

"Death," she answered. She held herself even tighter, but this might be more out of sadness than fear. "A curse is killing every member of my family. I'm in danger, Mr. Risk, and you're the only one who can help."

"And what makes you think the deaths—"

"Two hours ago, my brother was trampled by an elephant!" she interrupted him. "That sort of accident doesn't happen every day."

"Sit, please." Mr. Risk gestured toward his most comfortable office chair, stuffed with Icelandic eiderdown and upholstered with fabrics imported from Mongolia.

This was the case he'd been waiting for, courtesy of a jarringly beautiful woman who needed his help. He waited until she sat before he said, "Ma'am, I'd be willing to take your case."

"Really? You mean it?"

He sat on the sofa next to her, back straight, chin high. He was about to tell her something very important, and he needed to make sure he appeared trustworthy. He waited until she looked him right in the eyes. "First of all, you've come to the right place."

Rebecca nodded.

"I've faced many cases such as yours, so I hope you're aware of my expertise in these matters. Are you? Are you aware?"

"I know your reputation, Mr. Risk. In fact, I read about you in the paper last week. You stopped a diamond smuggler, if I remember correctly. I believe he was posing as a snake charmer."

Mr. Risk nodded in recognition, though he knew that the newspapers severely embellished the whole affair. It had taken him a mere hour to question the pet store owner, follow the clues to the wharf, and apprehend the thief and all six of his men. It was a fairly easy adventure, especially with Abdul by his side.

"You did an amazing job, obviously," Rebecca continued. "But this is clearly a different matter. This is… supernatural."

Mr. Risk remained in his seat, waiting for the woman to once again look him in the eyes. "Listen to me, please. If I'm going to take your case, you have to promise that you'll trust my judgment and do what I say. Alright?"

"Yes, Mr. Risk."

"Good. Because the first thing I need you to do is forget that curse nonsense. I've seen supernatural events of all kinds, and they are never, ever supernatural. They always have a rational explanation."

"I'm sorry, Mr. Risk," she said, "but not this time. This time is…"

Her voice cut off when Abdul shoved a glass of water in her hands. She downed half of it in seconds.

"Without knowing the full story," Mr. Risk explained, "I would wager that there are two possible explanations: either there's been a string of unrelated yet terrible accidents, or someone is plotting against your family and its business. Now, please, tell me everything."

Rebecca set her glass onto the table, accidentally knocking over her purse as she did. It flopped to the side and made a strange hiss noise. Confused, Rebecca reached for the buttons to pull open the flap, when something shot out of the purse.

Mr. Risk sprung into action. Even before he knew what it was, he knew he had to stop it. He leapt over his teak coffee table from Nairobi and snatched the projectile out of the air before it could reach Rebecca.

He looked down and saw a snake writhing around in his hand. Thankfully, he'd caught it by the neck, so its long fangs couldn't reach him. Its tail flopped around wildly.

Abdul ran to his boss, his machete held high.

"No," Mr. Risk commanded. "Bring me a box so we can contain it."

Abdul nodded, though his expression showed slight disappointment that he was prevented from springing into action. He set the machete on the coffee table, causing Rebecca's eyes to widen at the large weapon placed right in front of her.

Abdul grabbed a thick wicker basket from a shelf. That basket had been made by a family of farmers in Ohio who thought their scarecrow was possessed. After Mr. Risk helped them realize that the scarecrow was merely a neighbor in disguise, they'd given him this basket, promising that it was more durable and impenetrable than metal. Mr. Risk didn't quite believe the claim, but he knew it would be a suitable container for a deadly animal.

The animal in question had lost some of its anger, but it was still hissing little specks of venom onto Mr. Risk's shirt. He could tell by the unique black, orange, and purple stripes that this was a Great Rhodesian Dung Viper, one of the rarest and deadliest snakes in the world. Someone must have spent a lot of time and money to bring one here. Mr. Risk knew that this case was even more intriguing than he'd first thought.

Abdul held the lid open as Mr. Risk shoved the viper into the basket. Abdul slammed the lid shut, secured it, and placed the basket gently on the floor. It continued to move as the snake violently slammed itself against the walls of its new prison.

Mr. Risk turned back toward Rebecca, who was sitting in stunned silence. "One bite would've killed you in minutes."

That was enough to pull Rebecca out of her shock. She jumped to her feet and yelled, "*Now* do you understand? I'm cursed!"

"It sure seems like it," Abdul muttered.

Mr. Risk gave a short warning glare to his assistant. He knew that, despite all their adventures together, Abdul was always more prone to believing in the supernatural.

The box shook on the ground as the trapped snake tried in vain to escape.

"Please go on," Mr. Risk implored.

Rebecca took a deep breath. Then slowly, she began her story. "Garvey Circus was founded by me and my four brothers. It was my oldest brother Lionel's idea. The circus was his passion project, and the rest of us went along with it because of his sheer enthusiasm. All he wanted to do was travel the country and make people happy, one crowd at a time.

"It took us about a year to get everything started, but once we had our crew and our animals, we were… Well, we were the best. Exotic animals, trapeze artists, enough clowns for *two* clown cars."

"Wow," Abdul muttered under his breath.

"We were huge. Every year was more profitable than the last… Until this year. My brother Lionel was sorting through our finances when he realized that someone on our staff was stealing from the company. A little bit here, a little bit there, but the missing money added up. Lionel and I had to interview every worker, but we found our thief: Madame Rita, the fortune teller."

Rebecca reached for her purse. She opened it very slowly, checking that it was snake-free, and then pulled out a photo. She handed it to Mr. Risk.

He studied the image of an extremely old woman dressed in bright fabrics and dangling jewelry. She was hunched over a crystal ball.

"This is her," Rebecca explained. "She's a genuine soothsayer from the mountains of Carpathia. She can commune with the spirit world. Trust me. I've seen her in action."

Mr. Risk had dealt with dozens of fortune tellers like Madame Rita. They always put on a good show, but they were never actually speaking to the dead. Their only real power was the ability to read people, to understand what customers want to hear. They were con artists plain and simple. Of course, Mr. Risk didn't say any of that. He simply waited for Rebecca to continue.

"We had to fire Madame Rita," she said. "We were in Wichita at the time, and Lionel confronted her in front of everyone. He told her to pack up and leave. I guess he wanted to make an example out of her, doing what he did in front of everybody. That was… a mistake. Rita made a huge spectacle out of it. She dove to her knees and begged for Lionel to forgive her. When he wouldn't, she grabbed his hand and cursed him. In front of everybody, she said that Lionel was going to die, and that everyone in the Garvey line would soon join him.

"And that night, there was a death, but it wasn't Lionel. While Madame Rita was packing her belongings, she had a heart attack and died. I guess the shock of losing her job was just too much for her. That, or her curse had drained the last of her energy. Either way, she was gone."

Rebecca stopped. She looked as if her words were giving her physical pain. Once again, she glanced at the box on the floor. The snake had stopped thrashing around. Now the box was completely still.

"After that, the accidents started," she said. "Just two days after the old woman's death, Lionel was mauled by a lion."

"I'm sorry to hear that," Mr. Risk said, more as encouragement to continue than as a genuine moment of sympathy. He understood the tragedy in Rebecca's words, but right now, he was focusing on the facts, the specifics, not on the emotions.

"My second brother Peter died after that," she continued. "He was trampled by horses while he was moving equipment. It was horrible. And those horses loved him. They really did. Such peaceful creatures, but it was like… something awful took hold of them, just for a few minutes. After they killed Peter, they just trotted back to their pen as if nothing had happened."

"And when was this?"

"About two weeks ago." She wiped her eyes. "And then tonight… I guess it was my brother Patrick's turn. He had taken over ringleader duties after Lionel's death, and he had just opened our show when… Well, I already told you about the elephant."

Mr. Risk rubbed his chin. "Three animal-related deaths."

"Three so far," she said. "And now it's just me and my youngest brother Ronald. I know that either one of us is next."

"Perhaps," Mr. Risk said.

"No! It's a certainty. That snake in my purse… Isn't that proof enough? I live in constant fear."

"And that's where I come in," Mr. Risk said reassuringly. "My lack of fear will allow me to do what you cannot. It'll get to the bottom of this."

She smiled at his words, but it was a thin, forced smile.

Mr. Risk considered her story. Then he asked, "And what is your brother Ronald's main job?"

"Animal trainer," she answered instantly. "Though we've both taken on more responsibilities in recent weeks."

"And do your trust Ronald?"

"Of course! He's my brother."

"So you trust him completely?"

"Yeah…" she said slowly. Then, more assertively, she added, "Yes."

"With your other brothers gone, does that mean that you and Ronald are the only owners of your family circus?"

She nodded.

"And if an 'accident' happens to befall you, then Ronald will have the circus all to himself?"

Rebecca fidgeted uncomfortably in her chair. "I know what you're thinking, Mr. Risk, and you're wrong."

"What am I thinking?"

"You're thinking that Ronald is training our animals to bump us off one-by-one so he can take over the circus."

"It's a logical explanation."

"There's just one problem," she said. "Garvey Circus is going under. Ticket sales have shrunk by more than half because of all the bad publicity. No one wants to visit a circus where people *die*. And with Patrick's death happening in front of a whole crowd, I doubt that we'll have any customers tomorrow. Not to mention our staff, who are all ready to quit. I don't think our little circus can survive."

"I see." Mr. Risk stood up. "It looks as though there's only one thing we can do."

"What's that, boss?" Abdul asked.

"We're going to the circus."

Mr. Risk, Abdul, and Rebecca arrived at the circus at sunset. Of course, the sun was hidden by storm clouds all day, so nightfall didn't make much difference. The rain was still steady and strong, pelting against the trailers and tents. The circus lights were already turned off.

The trio passed by workers in and out of costume, carrying boxes and keeping their heads down. A few glanced at Rebecca and her new friends, but no one acknowledged them.

"They're ready to quit," Rebecca whispered. "Every last one of them. And honestly, I don't blame them."

The animal cages were lined up under a long awning that stretched along the back of the open field with trailers on either side. Most of the animals were already asleep, but a few casually roamed around their cages. None of them looked ready to attack.

"The main tent is right there." Rebecca pointed to the largest structure in the field, a red and yellow striped tent that looked sad with all its lights out. "That's where Patrick…" She couldn't finish her sentence.

When they entered the tent, they saw a tall, thin man addressing about a dozen people gathered in front of him. This was Ronald. "I understand your concerns, but please, there is absolutely nothing to worry about. Right now, my sister is talking to someone who can help us. As soon as she gets back…"

"Ronald!" Rebecca called.

Ronald spun around to see his sister. "Back already?"

"This is Mr. Risk and his associate," Rebecca introduced. "He promised to stop the curse."

Ronald looked at him strangely, then forced a smile. "Pleased to meet you." He turned back toward his group of workers. "Men? We have everything under control. Just get back to your trailers and we'll have a meeting in the morning. And again, there is nothing to be afraid of."

A few members of the crowd whispered their disapproval. A few more groaned. As a group, they all walked out the back entrance of the tent. The only worker to stay was one of the acrobats, a woman, who stood at the edge of the tent and watched Mr. Risk search for clues.

He started in the center ring, where Patrick's blood still stained the ground. Meanwhile, Rebecca and Abdul followed Ronald outside of the tent to inspect the elephant cages.

It didn't take long for Mr. Risk to find something peculiar on the ground. At first, he thought it was a scrap of purple fabric, probably from one of the clowns' outfits. Upon closer inspection, he saw that it was a pile of crushed flower petals, light purple with speckles of red and blue. They sat on the ground, at the exact spot where Patrick Garvey had been trampled. He picked up several of the petals and slid them into his breast pocket.

The flowers were definitely a clue, though he'd need to do some research to discover their true significance.

He continued his search, studying the elephant footprints and blood stains. Before he could find anything else, a hand grabbed him from behind.

He spun around, suddenly looking into a pair of beautiful green eyes. This was the acrobat, the only worker who hadn't left the tent. Her long black hair hung in thick waves down to her waist. She wore a one-piece body suit covered in fake jewels, reflecting tiny sparks of light whenever she moved her shapely body.

"Excuse me," she said. "You're… a detective, right?"

"Something like that," Mr. Risk answered.

She shook his hand. "I'm Valora, acrobat and tightrope walker. Do you need any help?"

While Mr. Risk had been struck by Rebecca's beauty, he was absolutely floored by Valora's. There was something magnetic about her, as if her eyes were drawing him closer with the secrets they held. From her raven hair and olive skin, he couldn't tell what country she was from, though her voice sounded generically American.

She intrigued him. He needed to focus on his work, but he wasn't opposed to spending just a bit more time with Valora. "I could always use the help," he said. "Did you see anything?"

"I saw it all. The giant, gray feet slamming down, Patrick getting stomped into a puddle." She stared at her feet. They were still standing in the spot where he'd died. "And I saw the others, too. I was outside Ronald's trailer when the lion attacked Lionel. I was behind the horses when they trampled poor Peter. I saw each death, Mr. Risk. Just terrible."

"You know my name."

"Your reputation proceeds you," she said. "The man without fear, right?"

"At each of the deaths, did you see anything… strange?"

"I'd say getting torn apart by a lion is strange," she answered. "But I know what you're getting at, and no. I don't think anyone is behind this. I think these were all terrible accidents."

"You don't believe in the curse?"

Valora shook her head. "Of course not. Madame Rita was a crackpot with no special powers. People are just scared."

"And you're not?"

She leaned closer. A lock of her black hair fell onto his shoulder and she whispered into his ear, "You're not the only one without fear, Mr. Risk. Let me show you."

She ran toward the ladder leading up to the tightrope and started climbing. She reached the small platform on top, then yelled down toward Mr. Risk. "This is what I would've done if tonight's show hadn't been cancelled!"

She spread out her arms and began her slow, graceful walk across the tightrope. Her face didn't show a hint of fear. There was a small net below her, but if she fell, she'd have to land on it just right... or else she'd break her neck.

Mr. Risk watched her stop in the center of the tightrope and then do two graceful flips without falling. He studied her face to see if she showed any hints of fear. She was too high up for him to be certain, but it looked as if she was completely at peace forty feet off the ground.

She spread her arms to either side and then continued walking the rest of the rope. When she reached the platform on the other side, she finally looked down at Mr. Risk. "Impressed?"

"Very," he shouted up to her.

"Great," she called back. "Would you like to give it a try?"

He was here to find information, not prove his fearlessness.

"Don't tell me you're too... *afraid*!" Valora shouted. Her voice echoed through the tent.

Mr. Risk smiled. "Not at all," he said. He knew she was goading him into joining her, but he gave in, anyway. In seconds, he had climbed the ladder opposite Valora and stood on a platform forty-ish feet high. "So what should I do? Just walk across?"

"That's it," Valora answered.

"And you get *paid* for this?" he joked. Then he took a deep breath, steadied his mind, and began walking one foot in front of the other. When he was about halfway across the tightrope, he waved to Valora. "Would you like to meet in the middle?"

"I thought you'd never ask." She leaned down and adjusted the screws connecting the tightrope to the platform. "Because of the extra weight," she explained. Then she spread out her arms again and began to walk toward Mr. Risk in the middle of the rope.

After just a few steps, Mr. Risk knew that something was wrong. The tightrope was starting to sag under their combined weight. The threads of the rope itself creaked. And then, there was a loud snap and the rope gave way.

When normal people fall to their deaths, they're usually too panicked to think of a way to save themselves in the split second before it's too late. For Mr. Risk, a split second was all he needed. As the rope fell out from under him, he allowed himself to fall backward, perfectly straight. He raised his arms over his head. At that angle, he was able to grab onto the rope and swing on it like Tarzan. Soon, he found himself dangling mere feet off the ground. He hopped down to safety.

Once again, Mr. Risk's level head had kept him alive. If he had a single moment of panic, he wouldn't have had the wherewithal to grab onto that rope. Any other man would've plummeted to a horrible, bloody death, but not him.

Now that he was safe from falling, he looked over to the opposite platform to see if Valora was still okay. Right away, he saw that the platform was empty. She wasn't there.

Then he looked down. Valora should've fallen into the net. It was directly below where she had been standing on the tightrope. Somehow, she missed. Her body lay on the ground, head and arms twisted to the side.

He called to her, but when she didn't move, he knew that Garvey Circus had just suffered another fatal accident.

"What's going on?" That was Ronald Garvey's voice. He had just run in, with Abdul and Rebecca right behind. He skidded to a stop in front of Valora's body. He whimpered and then backed away. It looked like he was too overcome with shock to say or do anything, but then he forced his expression to go blank.

"Is she…?" Rebecca whispered.

Ronald reached down to touch Valora's neck. He felt her skin for a long moment, then said, "She's dead." He turned toward Mr. Risk and glared. "What did you do?"

"The rope snapped," Mr. Risk answered.

"He didn't do anything," Rebecca chimed in. "It was the curse!"

Abdul bowed his head.

Ronald stood back up. "I'm afraid she's right, Mr. Risk. There's no use denying it anymore."

Mr. Risk needed to convince them that giving in to superstition would only get in the way of finding the real answers. Unfortunately, he didn't know how to change their minds. Aside from a few unidentified flower pedals, he didn't have any proof to show them. He decided to let them think what they wanted.

Ronald walked to Mr. Risk and looked him right in the eyes. "Look after my sister, will you? I need to… tend to another tragedy." He nodded in Valora's direction.

"I understand."

Rebecca grabbed her brother's arm. "But Ronald…"

He shook her away. "Don't. Just stay safe for the night. Tomorrow, we'll talk about closing the circus for good."

BACK AT HIS HOUSE, MR. RISK SCANNED HIS LIBRARY WHILE ABDUL WATCHED after Rebecca. He knew exactly what book to look for, but he didn't tell them yet. It was never wise to share a theory before it was fully formed.

"A-*ha!*" he shouted as he pulled out an ancient-looking book called *Plant Life of Eastern Europe*. He set it on the table and flipped through its crumbling pages. About halfway through the book, he found the page that he wanted. Then he pulled out the flower pedals from his breast pocket to compare them with the book's illustration.

Rebecca leaned over to look. "What is it?"

Mr. Risk pointed toward the illustration, which showed a small, purple flower that matched perfectly with the pedals in his hand. "*This* is your curse," he said.

"Huh?"

"The *faunus infuriorna*. It doesn't have a common name because it's not a common flower. It grows in the mountains of Carpathia and it's extremely dangerous. Its aroma has a very specific effect on most animals." He pointed toward the page's second illustration, a black-and-white line drawing of a villager being torn apart by wolves. "Basically, this flower makes animals attack."

Rebecca gasped.

"Miss Garvey," he said, "look inside your purse. I have a feeling you'll find some pedals of your own."

Sure enough, she pulled out two purple pedals with the same markings.

"Now do you see?" Mr. Risk asked. "I found this flower on the exact spot where the elephant killed your brother. I wouldn't be surprised if the flower was also near Lionel and Peter when they died. This is the source of your problems. It has nothing to do with a gypsy curse."

"Of course it does!" Rebecca argued. "It's from Carpathia, right? That's where Madame Rita is from. It must be her calling card. She leaves it at the scene of every death."

"Rebecca, do you know for a fact that Madame Rita is dead?"

"Yes! I saw her body myself. I helped bury her."

Abdul stepped forward. "Master? What about the woman?" He meant Valora. Her death had no connection to animals of any kind.

"Good point," Mr. Risk answered. "That's the one piece that doesn't fit."

"The *one* piece?" Rebecca shouted. "Even if your theory is true and Madame Rita is completely unconnected, we still don't know who is behind the flower pedals."

"It's only a matter of time," he replied. "But for now, let's act on the theory that someone other than a gypsy ghost wants your family dead. Agreed?"

Rebecca took a moment to compose herself. It was only natural. He waited for her to respond. He had several theories clicking through his brain, but he didn't want to overwhelm her with even more information.

Slowly, she nodded. "That has to be it. Mr. Risk, I think I believe you."

He smiled. "It's simple. Without panic and emotions fogging my mind, I'm able to quickly understand even the most outlandish situations. You would've figured it out eventually."

"I'm not so sure," she countered. "But… Valora. If there is no curse, then why did the rope snap?"

From the corner of the room, Abdul cleared his throat. It was his way of showing agreement. He clearly still believed in the curse.

"We'll figure it out," Mr. Risk promised. "I have a feeling that if we find out more about her death, we will discover who the killer really is."

Abdul pushed his large body out of his chair, readying himself for what Mr. Risk was surely going to say next.

"We must return to the circus at once," Mr. Risk said. "Things are about to get very dangerous, Miss Garvey, so I need you to stay behind."

"But…"

"Don't worry. You'll be safe here, I assure you. It's better for everyone if you wait until we return."

She opened her mouth to argue with him, but the words never came out. Instead, she nodded in silent agreement.

"Abdul? Are you ready?"

Abdul nodded and walked back into the rain.

Mr. Risk looked once more at his young client, smiled reassuringly, and left her to wait for their return in the safety of his study.

A MERE TEN MINUTES LATER, MR. RISK AND ABDUL RETURNED TO THE CIR-cus, this time without announcing their arrival. They'd left Rebecca in the safety of the house, having warned her not to open the door for anyone except them.

Rather than go through the main entrance, the two men circled around the back of the field, past the animal cages, and stopped in front of a row of parked trailers. Mr. Risk walked by each one, reading the names on the doors, until he stopped in front of Ronald's trailer.

"Why here, master?"

"Just trust me, okay?" He put his finger up to his lips, *shh*ing Abdul, and then knelt under the trailer's back window so he could listen in. Abdul did the same.

At first, all they heard was Ronald's voice from inside the trailer. He sounded agitated and angry, though they couldn't make out his exact words. Then a second voice came in, a woman's voice. She had a thick, Eastern European accent.

Abdul's eyes widened. "Madame Rita," he mumbled.

"Perhaps," his boss said. "Now just listen."

Slowly, Mr. Risk could make out a few phrases, each one painting a very damning picture of Ronald and the woman:

"The snake was supposed to kill her."

"Maybe we didn't use enough pedals."

"We'll get her tonight. I promise."

"And what about the detective guy?"

"We'll kill him, too."

This conversation confirmed most of Mr. Risk's suspicions. Ronald was plotting against his family. He had teamed up with… someone. And they used flower pedals to stage their murders.

He leaned closer to the window, straining to hear more of the conversation, but the woman started to whisper. Perhaps she realized that there were eavesdroppers.

For about a minute, the woman with the accent whispered something to Ronald. Then there was silence for a long moment, until the woman said, "I'll go find her."

The trailer's front door shot open, and the mysterious woman ran out. Mr. Risk peered around the corner just in time to see a tall, hunched figure in gypsy clothes hurry into the distance. She looked exactly like the photo of the fortuneteller, though a veil obscured her face.

"Madame Rita," Abdul whispered again.

"I'm starting to understand," Mr. Risk whispered to his assistant. "Run back home as fast as you can. Protect Rebecca from that woman. I'll stay here and have a talk with Ronald."

"Yes, master." He raced away.

Mr. Risk charged into the single-room trailer, but it was empty. He looked around, but there was no place for a full-grown man to hide. He didn't understand. He knew that Ronald was in here, and the only way out was the front door.

Then he noticed that a small window in the back was left open. He ran to the window and looked out. No one was there. He was about to turn and leave when he heard a noise directly above him. Ronald had climbed out the window and onto the roof. Mr. Risk had no idea why the man did that.

He slammed his palm against the ceiling. "I know you're up there, Ronald."

"Yes, Mr. Risk," the man called down. "We heard you coming. I'm safe up here. Unfortunately, you're not so lucky."

Before Mr. Risk could ask why, Ronald threw a handful of flower pedals through the window and back into the trailer. Several of them stuck to Mr. Risk's still-wet dress shirt.

"What's your plan, Ronald? I know you murdered your brothers."

"Maybe," he said. "Maybe not. Maybe I'm going to kill Rebecca and take over the circus myself. *With* the help of my new business partner."

He was talking about the foreign woman who had just left.

Mr. Risk was done talking through the ceiling. He needed to get out of this trailer and confront Ronald face-to-face, but when he opened the front door, he saw four blue eyes staring back at him. Two African lions were standing right outside. They sniffed the air and then crouched down into attack position. Mr. Risk slammed the door shut.

"Nice try," Ronald called down. "Now do you understand why I'm on the roof? You see, my partner and I heard you coming, so she released the lions on her way out. And I gave you the last of our flowers. It's only a matter of time before the lions break their way in. Good luck."

Mr. Risk peered outside the tiny window at the top of the door. He could see the prowling animals, their shadows stretched behind them. They sniffed the air and growled at each other. The way they circled the trailer reminded Mr. Risk of the pack of sharks that had once surrounded him off the coast of Peru. He had narrowly escaped with all his limbs attached, and this should be no different.

He didn't know what he would do to fight them off, but he was confident that a plan would come to mind. And if it didn't, if they tore him apart, then this would be his last adventure. Because he was unafraid of death, the thought meant very little to him.

Slowly, one of the lions approached the front door and began to claw against the thin wood. It yowled. A wide crack began to form, widening with each lion swipe. It wouldn't be long before the door cracked in two.

Ronald looked through the back window, peering upside down from the roof. His face was completely in shadow, but Mr. Risk could still make out an evil smile. "Sorry I have to leave," the man said. "But you're a professional. I'm sure you can figure out a way to escape with your life."

He disappeared from the window, but Mr. Risk knew he was still close enough to hear him. "Ronald!" he called as the lions continued ripping into the door. "You won't get away with this! Even if you kill me, I still have evidence linking you to all the murders."

His face reappeared in the window. "What evidence is that?"

The lions had cracked open the door wide enough for one of them to stick its snout into the trailer. It roared so loudly that Mr. Risk had to raise his voice. "I'm not telling you what the evidence is. It's safe in a wicker basket in my house, and you're not going to find it."

"Watch me!" Ronald shouted. Then he was gone. Mr. Risk could hear him jump off the trailer's roof and run away.

By now, the door was mostly splinters. In seconds, the lions would be able to break inside. Mr. Risk looked around for anything he could use. He didn't need a weapon, because even a man as strong as Mr. Risk wouldn't be able to take on two lions in such a small space. The only thing he needed was something to mask the flower smell.

The first lion pushed its whole body into the trailer. Its eyes locked on Mr. Risk. The second lion was just behind.

Mr. Risk grabbed the only object on the shelf behind him: a spray can. He didn't have time to read the label, but anything in a spray can had to be useful. He sprayed it all over himself, choking on the fumes.

It was bug spray.

As the lions stopped roaring and started coughing, Mr. Risk calmly walked between both of them and right out the door. It took a few seconds, but the lions followed. They prowled down the trailer's steps, still staring at Mr. Risk. They kept snarling, but their mouths looked more natural, a sign that they'd gotten over the effects of the *faunus infuriorna*. That was good. Now they were just regular animals again, and Mr. Risk knew exactly how to handle them.

He stood straight up, making himself as tall as he could. He stared straight into the first lion's eyes and waited. If the lion saw any fear on his face, it would attack. If it didn't, then it would walk away.

Man and animal stared each other down for nearly a minute, before both lions bowed their heads and approached him, one on either side. They obediently followed Mr. Risk toward their cages. He waved one arm and both animals crawled inside and peacefully allowed him to lock them back up.

He was safe. Now, he needed to rush back home and find Ronald and his strange business partner before anything happened to Rebecca.

LIGHTNING CRACKLED THROUGH THE AIR. MR. RISK RAN ALL THE WAY BACK to his house. It took him mere minutes, despite the rain. His suit clung to his body and his normally neat hair was matted against his head. Thankfully, the rain had washed away any traces of the *faunus infuriorna*, but it also left him cold and uncomfortable.

He ran through his front door, which was already wide open. Abdul and Ronald were inside, wrestling on the ground. Rebecca wasn't there. Neither was Ronald's mysterious partner.

Abdul had used his superior strength to pin the much-smaller man on the ground. Ronald jabbed and punched at Abdul. He acted like one of his wild animals.

It looked like Abdul was going to easily win the fight, but Ronald pulled out a pocketknife from his sock and jabbed Abdul in the forearm. The hulking manservant tumbled backward, pushing his body off the sofa to steady himself.

"Stop!" Mr. Risk shouted. "Abdul, it's no use. Ronald won." He stepped closer to the two men. With a quieter voice, he said, "Ronald, if we give you all the evidence we have against you, you and your partner promise to leave us and Rebecca alone?"

"How about this? I'll tell you everything I know about where Rebecca was taken, and you can go there and deal with my partner yourself."

"Agreed. Abdul, please give Mr. Garvey the evidence."

"Evidence, master?"

Mr. Risk nodded toward the wicker basket in the corner. The snake had probably given up on its escape plan, because the basket didn't move.

At first, Abdul looked confused. Then he nodded in understanding and stood up. He picked up the basket and brought it back to Ronald.

A dark, triumphant smile crossed Ronald's face as he clutched the basket close to his chest, completely unaware that a deadly viper was in his hands. "This is everything you have against me, right?"

"Correct."

"You promise?"

"I promise," Mr. Risk said. "Now where did your partner take Rebecca?"

Ronald laughed maniacally. "I honestly don't know. When I got here, they were already gone. See ya!"

"Wait!" Mr. Risk called out.

"Nope. A deal's a deal. I told you everything I knew. Now I'm out of here." Holding the basket like a baby, he raced out the door.

Mr. Risk and Abdul exchanged glances. "Well, Abdul, how long do you think it'll take him to open that basket?"

Abdul started to answer, but he was cut off by Ronald's loud, horrible scream just outside. "Not very long," he said.

Thanks to this species of snake and its potent venom, Mr. Risk knew that Ronald would no longer be a problem for them. They had just taken out the mastermind behind this nefarious plan. That just left the matter of finding Rebecca and saving her from the woman in the gypsy clothes.

Mr. Risk scanned the room for signs of Rebecca. He replayed the timeline in his head. Rebecca was here alone. Abdul came back first. Then the mysterious woman. Then Ronald. Ronald claimed that he didn't know where Rebecca was, and Mr. Risk believed that. She was gone before he got here. That just left the question: What did Abdul see?

"Was Rebecca here when you got back?"

"No, master," Abdul said, hanging his head as if he'd made a grave mistake. "I returned and the house was empty. I looked in every room, and no one was there. Then I came downstairs and Ronald attacked me."

"And that's when I came in," Mr. Risk finished for him. "I doubt that Rebecca would leave on her own. My best guess is that she was taken while you were searching the house. Perhaps she was in a part of the house where you didn't look."

He gasped. "The roof! I heard noises but thought it was the storm."

"It seems like everyone's climbing on roofs today," Mr. Risk muttered. "Let's check it out. Fast!"

The two men raced up three flights of stairs. The roof was accessible only from an attic door. Mr. Risk pushed the door open and slowed down so he could walk onto the sloped roof without falling. Abdul was right behind.

Their hunch was right. Rebecca was up here, standing on the edge with her hands in the air. And Ronald's partner, the murderess behind a veil, pointed a gun at her.

Mr. Risk and his servant had just escaped from a fistfight downstairs, only to enter a standoff on the roof.

Rebecca glanced at Mr. Risk but pretended she didn't see anything. "Please don't do this," she told the gypsy.

"You know I have to," the gypsy said in a thick accent.

"No you don't!" Mr. Risk shouted. "Don't make a move… Valora."

The gypsy laughed once. Then she pulled the veil off her face. She had no more use hiding. Mr. Risk looked straight into Valora's beautiful green eyes.

Rebecca gasped. Abdul gasped, too, which was a very rare occurrence for him.

Valora was still alive. *She* was Ronald's partner in crime. She'd already murdered three people, though it would've been four if Mr. Risk had succumbed to her lions, and now she had a gun pointed at Rebecca.

Mr. Risk was too far away to disarm her, so he'd need to distract her, get her talking. "Valora, we thought you were dead."

"I know!" she said, her true accent even thicker now. "That was the plan. Actually, the real plan was to lure you to the tightrope, let you fall to your death, and blame it on the curse. But you survived, so I… adjusted. I landed on my net, like a professional would, but when I saw you swinging to safety, I jumped onto the floor and played dead. I figured that would get you off our trail."

"*Our* trail. You mean you and Ronald. The two of you used the *faunus infuriorna* to kill the other Garveys and take over the circus."

Valora started to clap. "Very good. I underestimated you, Mr. Risk."

"You're not the first," he retorted. "And I must commend you on a very clever plan. Though it all seems for nought, since Ronald is already dead."

Valora cackled like a witch. "Do you think I care one bit about Ronald Garvey? Wow. Maybe I *over*estimated you. I'm happy he's dead. Our relationship was entirely transactional. He thought we were taking over the circus together. The fool! I used him and… now I don't need him anymore."

"Then what do you want?" Rebecca shouted. She was standing so close to the edge, she couldn't stop herself from looking at the ground far below.

"Not much," Valora said. "Just revenge. You know, complete and total destruction for the family that killed my mother."

"Your… mother?" Rebecca whispered.

Valora cackled again. "My *mother*. Madame Rita. She was eighty! She worked for you for years, and you threw her out like trash!"

"She was stealing—"

"She was a good woman!" Valora screamed. For a second, she got a faraway look on her face. She stared at the dangling beads and bracelets on her wrist. "After she died, I knew I had to avenge her. And all it took was a little herb from the old country." She turned toward Rebecca. "Your brothers know what happens next."

"You monster!" Rebecca screamed.

Valora cackled proudly. Her plan was insane and wildly complicated, but somehow, it worked. She'd gotten exactly what she wanted, and now, all she had to do was watch Rebecca fall. Just one more act of violence and then everything would be complete.

As Valora started to push Rebecca over the edge, Mr. Risk sprang into action. He had no weapons and no plan. It was an impossible situation, but that had never stopped Mr. Risk before. He ran headlong across the roof and jumped onto Valora. And together, they both plummeted off the building.

The fall took less than a second, but that was all the time Mr. Risk needed to grab a tree branch on the way down. He collided against the tree. Hard. He was bruised but okay.

Valora wasn't so lucky. For the second time that night, she fell to her death, but this time, it stuck. When Mr. Risk looked down from the tree, all he saw was a bloody pile of veils and scarves.

By the time Mr. Risk climbed down the tree, Rebecca and Abdul had already reached the front yard. They stood by Valora's body. Rebecca even nudged it with her foot to make sure Valora was really dead.

She was.

And just a few feet away was another dead body. Ronald's. He lay next to the front porch, his face badly swollen. The wicker basket lay next to him. There was no sign of the snake, though Mr. Risk made a mental note to have Abdul search the premises in the morning.

Rebecca grabbed Mr. Risk by the arm. She looked like she was going to faint. "How did you know that it was Valora?"

"I wasn't certain," he answered. "But Valora's supposed death on the tightrope always seemed strange. Like you said, it didn't match the other murders. As soon as Ronald checked her pulse and said that she was dead, I had a feeling that he was lying, that the two of them were in cahoots."

Rebecca glanced at Ronald's body. "What happened to him?"

"Killed by the same snake that was meant to spell your doom. It was fitting."

The rain was beginning to slow. In a few minutes, it would stop completely and the storm would be over.

For the first time since she walked into his life, Rebecca smiled. It truly was a smile to behold, one that lit up the night in a way that Mr. Risk hadn't expected. She wasn't just beautiful; she was radiant. And yet... there was still a sliver of sadness. She was the last Garvey standing.

"You'll be okay," he told her.

"I know. I'm so grateful to be alive, but... I'll never get my brothers back." She breathed deeply. "And after everything that's happened, it looks like our circus will be closed forever."

"I wouldn't be so sure," he argued. "You're still here, and if you want to reopen, I'm sure you can. And this time, there will be nothing to be afraid of."

The End

ABOUT THE AUTHOR

EVAN PURCELL IS A SCREENWRITER AND NOVELIST, WITH TWO NEW HORROR films coming out later this year. His next ebook "Estelle Harrow" will be released this summer. It's a pulp mystery about a spunky medium who solves supernatural crimes with the help of her dead sister.

Read more about his travels and projects at EvanPurcell. blogspot.com or follow him on BlueSky @evancpurcell.

AN ILLUSTRATION FROM FRANK LESLIE'S ILLUSTRATED NEWSPAPER, 1897.
GAMBLERS ARE PLAYING FAN-TAN, A CHINESE GAME OF CHANCE, IN A PARLOR IN NEW YORK.

BY DALE ALEXANDER

I met Alfie Armstrong the day I moved into my new classroom after a disappointing summer. I remember specifically because it was just before all this happened. I was carrying boxes full of personal stuff I had taken home at the end of the last school year. I didn't think I'd be coming back, but here I was: the same curriculum, same coworkers, and the same old school year cycle. I felt like there was something reassuring about familiarity, I guess. It didn't really end up that way though.

I passed him in the hallway going opposite directions. I was struggling with the boxes. He was taller than me, and his district-issued work shirt hung from his shoulders like a kite abandoned in a high tree branch. Experiences creased his forehead, and his eyes were set deep in shadowy sockets.

I gave him a brief nod as he walked the other direction. He had a reserved look and a purpose in his step that made me unsure he'd want to launch into conversation with anyone just then. I made my way to my classroom and watched him disappear down an intersecting hallway, then reappear a second later and look both directions.

When he looked my way, he hesitated. I stood with my boxes balanced between my knee and the wall, fishing in my pocket for my key. I watched his internal debate, but eventually he must have found either the nerve or the desperation to approach me.

"Let me give you a hand," he said. He held the two boxes while I unlocked the door, then followed me in. He put them down on a desk and turned to me.

"Alfie Armstrong," he said, and extended a hand.

I shook it. "Mason Dell," I said. I teach English. Are you new here?"

"Yeah," he admitted. He studied the box he had just set down. "I'm trying to find the building services office. I'm supposed to meet a guy named Benson."

I knew Ray Benson well. He had been our head custodian for longer than my 12 years at the school.

"I can show you where that is. I'm headed that way to see if I can hunt up some coffee in the faculty lounge."

Alfie studied me with hesitance I couldn't place before finally consenting. New guy, I figured. New building, lots to acclimate to.

We walked down the main hallway passed the remaining blue and white (school colors, you know) posters celebrating last year's events and sports teams, all of which would soon be replaced with highlights from this upcoming fall. We passed the large window wall looking out on the practice field and saw the football team in the first of two practices that day. A challenge in August, even in Northern Illinois: Pain is just weakness leaving your body.

"Where are you from?" I asked, breaking what threatened to become an uncomfortable silence.

"Chicago originally," he said. "But I bounced around some."

"What brings you here?"

"The job," he admitted. "I got a little experience pushing a broom. The job market for a guy my age ain't what it used to be." He continued staring straight ahead.

I couldn't argue with him.

We turned left at the school's main intersection and passed the administration office. Alan Petrowski, the Dean of Students, was unlocking the door to walk in. We stopped, and I introduced Alfie, explaining our mission.

"Nice to meet you," Alan said, shaking hands. "Glad you're here."

Then, to me: "Surprised to see you back! But I'm glad you're here too." He smiled. "How's the novel coming?"

"Oh," I lied, "slowly. I'm not sure exactly where it's going."

Alan opened the door and stepped inside, turning on the light. "I'm sure you'll get it straightened out," he said. "That has been important to you for quite a while."

Alfie and I walked to the end of the hall and turned right. The first door we came to was the teacher's lounge.

"This is me," I said. "There's probably coffee if you want some."

"No, thanks."

"Suit yourself." I pointed. "Building services is down there at the end of the hall, on your left."

"Thanks. For your help. I . . . really appreciate it," he said, eyes studying the hallway.

"No sweat," I said. "Good to have met you. I'm sure I'll be seeing you again."

He turned and made his way down the hall while I flipped on the light to the teacher's lounge.

THE MIRROR PROBLEM STARTED SMALL, IN A WAY THAT MADE ME QUESTION IF it actually happened, the way you second guess if you remembered to turn off the oven or locked the back door when you go to bed. It can gnaw at you, but once you reassure yourself, it doesn't bug you anymore. I had no way of knowing how quickly it would escalate, how much it would make me question, or even how it would eventually involve Alfie Armstrong. At first, it seemed like just a trick played by my tired eyes.

I was brushing my teeth one night about a week after I had met Alfie Armstrong. School had started two days previously, and I was just getting to the part where introductory stuff ended, and real work began. By the end of that day, I was tired enough to prove it.

I squeezed Crest onto my Oral B and leaned against the pedestal sink as I went to work. After a few back and forths I stood upright and looked at myself in the mirror. Except, for a split second, it wasn't. At least it wasn't what I was doing. My elbow and shoulder moved back and forth, bristles rubbing the day off my front teeth, but for the blink of an eye, my reflection just didn't. The arm was still, and although I felt myself moving, felt the brush against my teeth and gums, for a beat – in the mirror – there was nothing. My reflection was frozen in time, and my brain recorded a disconnect that sent a shiver through me.

It felt like the closing seconds of a basketball game when your team is up by a pair and you're clock watching, time moving as slowly as it possibly can. You promise yourself you won't look, but in the end, you can't help it, and you happen to look up exactly as one second ticks off, and the clock looks frozen because that one second feels so long that you look away before it ticks to the next. To you in that moment, the clock isn't moving.

That was my arm. I was sure that's what had happened. I had felt my arm move, but the mirror had shown me that pause. I looked down and back up, and sure enough, my arm was moving as it should be, in exact harmony with what I felt.

I stopped brushing, stood upright, and let my hand drop to the sink's edge. I wasn't sure whether I felt relief or more confused by what had just happened. I moved my head back and forth. All appeared normal. I sighed and decided to let it go: A trick of tired eyes, no doubt. I raised my hand to continue the tooth brushing, and in the mirror, my reflection hesitated.

I had my hand to my mouth, brush on teeth, and I FELT it. I knew it was there because I tasted the mint. I felt the bristles. And THEN I saw my arm in the mirror complete the same motion. It was quick, like it was making up for lost time: It moved twice as fast as I had moved to show me my current state, and then it was in sync again with where I was.

I dropped the brush and stared at my reflection again for a long time, watching myself move. I was reading it 5x5. There was nothing wrong with the signal.

"FREDDIE! FREDDIE WHERE ARE YOU?" I WALKED THROUGH THE HOUSE DRIP-ping toothpaste onto my white t shirt, knowing full well where I'd find my son. Knocking on his bedroom door and getting no response, I opened it to find what I knew I would.

Freddie sat at his desk amidst what could only be referred to as the dumpster fire of his bedroom. Teenage boys are not, and have never been, known for their tidiness.

Freddie was a good-looking fourteen-year-old whose weight had not yet caught up with his height, and whose hair seemed to make up its own mind about what to do in the morning even though I know he planned it carefully. Dishes, wrappers, paper, and the detritus of numerous dollar-store whims covered every surface. His dirty clothes basket sat empty while half his floor was covered in already-worn clothing. The light was off, illumination coming only from various seizure-inducing flashes on his 36-inch gaming monitor. His fingers worked the buttons ferociously and he babbled into his headset mic.

My entry startled him and his head whipped around to face me.

"Come here," I said.

He looked at me wide eyed.

"Pause your game, or stop it, and come with me."

"I can't, Dad, it doesn't pause. We're battling. . . "

I wasn't going to let him finish that sentence. I didn't care what fantasy he was battling, when I was battling my sanity. I grabbed his headphones and pulled him by his shirt sleeve.

"Hey. . ." he protested. "Micah is going to die without. . ."

"He'll be right back Micah," I called as I pulled him out of his room and down the hallway toward the bathroom. "Don't die without him."

"Brush your teeth," I said when we arrived.

He looked at me like I'd grown an extra head.

"Just do it," I insisted, handing him his toothbrush.

"Dad, I brushed my teeth an hour ago."

I handed him the crushed tube of Crest as well. He rolled his eyes and turned on the faucet.

"What is this about?" he asked. "This is really weird. It reminds me of when. . ." He trailed off.

"When what?" I prompted.

He layered toothpaste on the bristles. "After mom died," he said after a minute.

I wasn't sure what to tell him. Did I admit what I had seen and sound even crazier? He was right. I had looked batshit crazy to him more than once in the time after his mother died. I realized I did need to care what he was battling, too.

The alternative was to lie to him. Something else I'd done more than once after his mother's death. And not something I wanted to repeat. I chose door C.

"It's. . . not like that. Please just humor your old man," I said. "I worry about you." Nonspecific, but entirely accurate. I decided I had passed that test.

He relented and brushed, not sure where to look. I felt slightly guilty as his gaze shifted among me, the mirror, and the sink. I, however, stared directly at the mirror the entire time, vigilant for discrepancies between him and his reflection while keeping my peripheral vision glued to him.

After a few minutes of lackluster, yet thorough brushing, he spit out his toothpaste then rinsed his brush off, dropping it into the sink afterward. His reflection obeyed all the rules.

"Ok?" He stared at me, both eyebrows drifting north. "Can I go now?"

I looked at the brush in the sink then back at him. His expression reminded me so much of his mother. When had he grown up so much?

"Yeah, go on," I said. "I hope you guys win."

He spun out of the bathroom and went back to killing zombies.

I stood, dissecting what had just happened. Should I try brushing my teeth again? Would that make things better or worse? After a few minutes I put Freddie's toothbrush back in the holder. I didn't need to poke this bear anymore tonight. I was freaked out enough.

I WOKE UP THE NEXT MORNING FROM FITFUL-AT-BEST SLEEP AND WALKED INTO the kitchen. Remarkably, my coffee maker timer had worked. It seemed to malfunction about 50% of the time – but I was too broke, or lazy, to replace it. Plus, pushing a button and waiting 10 minutes isn't that big of a deal. Right?

"Alexa, play my discovery mix." I hated the idea of AI but secretly loved that Amazon Music would pick out a bunch of stuff that fit my algorithm and package it for me in a weekly playlist. All that new music waiting to be discovered, and rarely did Amazon fall outside my wheelhouse.

A second or two passed and a familiar riff filled the kitchen. Dale Nixon's guitar belted out the first few chords of the song "Million Days" by punk rock icons Dag Nasty, and it immediately took me back in time.

"Wow, I haven't heard this one in years," I said out loud. Alexa seemed indifferent to my reminiscence. Amazon had won again though; It wasn't new to me, but it was great, and I had almost forgotten it.

I poured myself a mug of coffee and leaned against the counter, listening to the crunchy guitar, convincing myself that last night had been stress-induced hallucination. Mostly successful, I walked to the refrigerator. Stainless steel and covered in drawings and photographs from Freddie's first 14 years, it held memories of all flavors.

"Alexa, pause."

I released the letter from its clip and dropped it on the counter before reading it. I did this occasionally these past few months to remind myself why I had quit writing. I had received rejections before: hosts of them. It's something writers get used to. But this one had made it clear to me that I was sniffing up the wrong tree. The stark brutality of the rejection leaving no doubt in my mind that those who can, do. Those who can't, teach. So, I quit doing, and I went back to teaching: That, at least, I knew I was good at.

Mug in hand and letter returned to its prominent place on the fridge, I attempted to get ready for the day. I let the shower steam the mirror before I got in. I wasn't sure I wanted to look at it anyway.

Eventually I got out, dried off, and brushed my teeth. Done. Finishing it was more of a relief than I'd expected: like remembering something I hadn't known I had forgotten. Afterward, I realized, I hadn't shaved in a couple days, and I was starting to look like I belonged more on a Harley than in front of a classroom.

Full of newfound confidence after the successful teeth brushing, I pulled out my razor, lathered up, and set to work. I did the bulk of the job from memory: a 47-year-old man who has never worn a beard knows the contours of his own face intimately. But after nicking myself twice on my throat, I relented.

I reached up and wiped the still-fogged mirror enough with my bare hand to create a ragged window dead center, just large enough to finish the job, which I did without further incident. Victory. I toweled off my face and hustled to my bedroom.

I started to dress, but realized that in my victorious haste, I had left the razor and shaving cream on the vanity, and the mirror open. Casually I walked back to the bathroom to clean up. When I closed the cabinet, my reflection was shaving.

A riptide of adrenaline pulled me under: My skin flushed, and I instantly popped a sweat on my forehead and neck. Numbness surged from the crown of my head to the tips of my toes, and the towel I still held wrapped around my waste dropped, as my digits became useless. I stood naked watching my mirror-self shave while both of my hands hung like seaweed at my sides.

This wasn't happening.

I hurried to the kitchen, leaving the towel on the floor, and poured myself a shot from the bottle of Tullamore DEW in the cabinet next to the refrigerator. I drank it off and poured one more, which I carried to the living room. I stared at the wall for a moment, sipping. Then a thought hit me.

I walked to the television - essentially a giant mirror. It delivered no surprises. Just a naked man, drinking whiskey from a glass tumbler at 7 am on a Tuesday. I moved my arm, and my reflection followed. I moved my leg, and my reflection followed. Everything in its place as it should be. And I mean everything.

The first shot of booze began to do its job, chasing the adrenaline for now. I sighed deeply and slammed the remaining whiskey. To my relief, my reflection drank with me. No one, under those circumstances wants to drink alone.

I returned to the kitchen and put my glass in the sink, pausing to think a moment.

"Fuck it." I ran a little water in the tumbler and hustled back to my bedroom to get dressed.

"You up?" I called to Freddie through his bedroom door on the way by.

He confirmed with something that sounded like English.

"Hurry up. We're going to be late."

I LACKED THE PATIENCE OR CONCENTRATION FOR TEACHING FIRST PERIOD THAT day. Luckily, I had handed out "Catcher in the Rye" to my juniors the day before. I handed them study questions for the first 3 chapters and instruct-ed them that today was for silent reading. Second period was my prep period so just had to make it through 55 minutes.

"Mr. D's hung over!" I heard a voice in the back of the classroom say as I walked forward handing out paper copies of study questions. I was still old school that way.

"No, I just don't trust you'll do it at home," I replied to raucous laughter.

Impressed that I had held it together as long as I did, I sat down at my desk and opened my laptop. I consulted the premiere authority on unknown ailments: Dr. Google.

Twenty minutes of rephrasing descriptions of what had happened to me yielded nothing comforting: no similar experiences described online. It was a lonely feeling, but not a surprising one; It wasn't anything I had heard of, not that I was an expert. I found several references to "Through the Looking Glass," and a few to the "Matrix" film series. But nothing helpful.

I spent the *next* twenty googling under the assumption that it was a hallucination. Those searches provided me with too many possibilities: brain aneurysm, partial stroke, macular degeneration, allergic reaction to something I ate, sleep deprivation, and on and on. It was useless. Any of them or none of them could be happening.

This was getting me nowhere. It had to be stress.

The bell rang, and the cattle stampeded.

"Questions are due tomorrow," I said to the backs of most of my students' heads as they exited.

After the last student left, I took off my glasses and pinched the bridge of my nose. My head pounded, and it wasn't even nine am. I longed for the Tullamore.

"You know, you can have them turn that in electronically, so you don't have to read teenage handwriting. These animals don't learn to write longhand anymore." Mark Crane leaned in my doorway. Mark taught English in the classroom right next to mine. He had a cliché late-40s hairline and a nose with its own zip code. His knit tie evoked the Regan era. He was probably my best friend on the faculty and shared my second period prep time.

"I'm aware."

"Why do you still hand out papers?" He approached and sat on the edge of my desk. "Jump into the 2000s, man."

"I'm old," I said. "I even have a landline." I waved a hand in his direction. "I don't wear knit ties, though."

He laughed and picked up the baseball from my desk, tossing it from hand to hand. "You look like shit."

"I'm aware of that too. I didn't sleep well."

"Again?"

"Different," I said. "I don't want to talk about it."

He put both hands up, his thumb securing the baseball to one palm; I won't say another word, he said without saying. Then: "Alan told me the novel's on hold."

"That's not what I told him." I sat back in my chair and crossed my arms over my chest. "I said I wasn't sure where it was going."

Shortly after my wife had died, I began a journal at the suggestion of my therapist. She explained that journaling can help grieving patients by aiding in processing emotions and tracking progress over time, among other benefits. I had not been acting entirely rational for a while and It wasn't fair to Freddie – or to myself. I gave journaling a try and wrote steadily for more than six months. I found it difficult at first but before long it became a part of my day I anticipated.

One day as I sat at my desk filling pages of my Moleskine, I found myself writing about writing. I wrote about how in high school, and while studying literature as an undergraduate and beyond, I regularly wrote for pleasure. Back then, although Hemingway I was not, I churned out a few decent stories and poems. A few had even made it into online literary journals here and there. When Freddie was born, my priorities changed, and I set it aside, sure I'd eventually get back to it.

I'm not sure where this memory had come from, or how it fit into processing feelings about my wife. Would writing fiction also be therapeutic, I wondered? A creative outlet and potential way to express emotions? I asked my therapist, and she told me it would be a great idea.

So for the next couple of years, I wrote furiously, ideas popping into my head became stories as I spent hours at my desk writing (longhand at first), and it helped. My behavior evened out. My grief didn't disappear, but I had created a coping mechanism that was effective.

After several successes placing short stories, I got deeply involved in writing a novel that felt like not only the next probable step, but also exactly what I needed to allow my writing career to blossom. I decided to take a year off from teaching and see if I could make a go of it. Until the letter came. Stark in its brutality, it reminded me of who I wasn't.

Crane chuckled and cocked his head at my hair-splitting.

"Ok I guess that means about the same thing." I admitted

"That's too bad," he said. "You were excited about it last spring"

"Yeah I don't know," I grabbed the baseball out of his hands. I knew he would drop it on my laptop. "I'm not sure writing's really for me. Takes up too much time, too much effort."

He shrugged and stood up. "You really do look like shit. I'm going for coffee. You coming?"

"Yes," I stood up and put my glasses back on. My vague reflection in my laptop matched my movements perfectly. It was stress. It was JUST stress. I needed to let that fact sink in and stop letting worrying about it be yet ANOTHER thing adding to my stress. That was way too meta. "Shame we don't have anything stronger."

Several days passed. I kidded myself as I walked in and out of my bathroom, past my television screen, down the windowed hallways at school, and looked in the rearview as I drove. I told myself I wouldn't think about it, but I thought about it. I told myself I was confident it would be perfectly normal each time, but I was terrified. Sometimes I even felt compelled to put myself in situations that would prove everything was fine. But they scared me every time. My breath caught whenever I anticipated seeing my reflection. I felt relief every time I didn't.

At the end of that week, I felt like I should attempt to bring things around to normal, for myself, but for Freddie as well. I knew how off I had been acting. I asked him if he wanted to go out for pizza. He grunted consent and lack of social agenda, so we hopped in the car and drove to Luigi's, a local place and a favorite for years.

Frank Sinatra crooned on the sound system as the hostess directed us to a table near the fireplace. I pulled menus from the condiment rack, and we both looked, as if we didn't know what we'd get: thin crust, pepperoni, bacon, extra cheese. It never varied. After a second, we dropped them onto the red and white checked tablecloth.

"How was school today?" Sure I'd just get a syllable or two, but not willing to sit in silence. We hadn't actually talked since the tooth brushing incident.

"It was school. How was yours?" His eyes didn't leave his phone.

I sat right next to him, but miles away. I cast around for something to say that wouldn't halt the conversation.

"Get you two something to drink?" The waitress interrupted.

I couldn't decide between annoyance and relief.

Freddie ordered a Coke, and I ordered a beer.

"Be right back with those," she said, and hustled to a different table.

"I need to take a leak," I told Freddie. I bumped my knee on the table's edge as I stood up to walk to the bathroom.

My anxiety amplified as I entered the bathroom and walked past the double-vanity sink, but nothing happened.

I finished my business and walked back to the sink to wash my hands.

When I saw my reflection brushing its teeth, I laughed at first. I dropped my head, braced myself on the counter, and took an extremely deep breath. The emotional nexus kicked my adrenal glands into high gear again. Somewhere downstream, they poured all they had into my blood, and I felt it crescendo with each heartbeat, surging a pulse at a time up through my body and into my head, where within a few seconds, I heard it in my ears like hurricane winds. My heart was a double kickdrum in a Metallica song.

I squeezed my eyes shut, sweat slamming out of my forehead and temples, dripping into the creases of my eyes. I white knuckled the countertop.

"No," I said out loud. "No, no, no." Then: "Ok, calm." I tried the breathing technique my therapist had suggested for panic attacks and anxiety shortly after my wife died: slowly, in through my nose for a count of four, hold it for a count of four, then exhale very slowly for a count of eight. Repeat as necessary.

I was oblivious when the door opened.

"Dad?"

Freddie's voice. I turned my attention to him, ignoring my peripheral vision.

"What do you see there?" I lifted one hand and pointed at the mirror. "What am I doing? What do you see? What do I look like?"

"Dad what's wrong?"

I hated him seeing this. Things had been so much better. Through hard work, I had regained control. The instability of the first year – my instability - after her death had been too hard.

"Just, what do you see?"

"Dad, you're freaking me the fuck out." Freddie rarely swore. I told him it was the language of the ignorant. But this time I got it. I was freaked the fuck out myself.

I closed my eyes and opened them. "Please."

Freddie hesitantly turned his head. "Us. You and me."

"What are we doing, though?"

"Dad!" Voice raised this time. "You promised this shit wouldn't happen again. Do you even remember what it was like for me?"

He was dead on. I released the counter and took one more deep breath, still staring at him. Slowly I stood up.

Drawing strength from somewhere – maybe Freddie's presence – I glanced back at the mirror. Like Freddie had said: the two of us just stood there. It took a minute to sink in.

I put my hand on his shoulder, still facing my reflection.

"I'm sorry, it's nothing. I just. . . thought I saw something that couldn't possibly be there."

"I can't do this."

I hadn't felt this low in a long time. The lie, unfortunately, came easy. "I'm ok. I'll be fine. I'm just really stressed out recently."

He stared at me with a visceral disbelief I couldn't measure. Then he turned and walked out. I got the pizza to go.

MONDAY MORNING, AFTER A WEEKEND COMPRISING TOO MANY BEERS AND TOO little sleep, I got up and got Freddie ready for school. I arranged for a substitute through our online system over the weekend. I needed a day to figure things out: a day when doctors' offices would be open and I could improve my state of mind.

I dropped him off and went home to make a call I hadn't wanted to make. But after Friday night, I saw no choice. I sat at my desk, a location I largely had abandoned since the letter had dropped on me in July. I had begun grading papers and doing lesson planning at the kitchen table this year, when I didn't do it at school.

The smallish desktop supported, in addition to my laptop, a few half-used notebooks, piles of manuscript printouts, various pens and sticky notes, and I even found an old dried out Starbucks cup. In the top drawer, I found Dr. Kristi Stenson's number, the therapist I had seen for a year after my wife died.

I called the office and asked for the first available appointment.

"I've got a 10 am on Tuesday the 27th," the receptionist said.

"That's almost 3 weeks from now." In my exasperation, I picked absently at the edge of my desk where some splinters had loosened over the years. One slid painfully under my thumbnail. I tried to pull it out and succeeded only in pushing it further. I swore quietly. Then: "Isn't there anything sooner?"

"There's no need for profanity, Mr. Dell. That's the first opening the doctor has available. I'd be glad to put you on a waiting list; in case something opens up."

"Huh? No, I was just," I shook my hand painfully. "Never mind. Yes. You can put me on the list. And please do call. I'd like to get in as soon as I can."

"I can put you in touch with a different therapist who might have openings sooner," she offered.

"No, I'll stick with Dr. Stenson. Thank you."

We hung up.

I walked to the kitchen and poured another cup of coffee, cringing as I looked at my reflection in the window above the sink. All normal. Of course it was. I was normal. I was fine.

I leaned back against the counter and saw the letter hanging on the refrigerator. In the time it took me to skim the letter, I relived all the time and energy I had spent, the hours of early mornings, late nights, days of research and reading, sweating the details, enjoying the process, creating something where there used to be a big fat nothing. All that time wasted: swept away with this one typed page. Better now, than later, I thought. Better after THAT much time and effort, than after twice as much.

I walked back to my cluttered desk and considered the piles of manuscript printouts: the fruits of those efforts. Setting my coffee cup down, I picked up the trash can and swept them all into it, emptying the surface, closing that chapter.

I FINISHED MY COFFEE SITTING ON THE COUCH FLIPPING THROUGH CHANNELS. I assured myself that calling the doctor had been a good step. I nodded as I thought about it. As the saying goes, healing begins when you make the phone call. I felt that acutely. I didn't want to go back into therapy. I worked hard the first year after my wife's death and I made progress. I thought THAT chapter was closed too. My current situation showed me differently.

The television lineup sucked, and when I found myself watching a rerun of a two-day-old Brewers game, the outcome of which I already knew, I realized it was time to move on. I looked at the clock: 10:30 am. I decided on a shower and a shave, and mirror be damned. The healing had begun.

After my shower, I walked to my bedroom to dress and passed the full-length mirror hanging next to my closet doors, only it wasn't me who passed: it was Alfie Armstrong.

I stood staring, wearing only my towel, water beading over flesh that blood had abandoned. My entire body felt chilled and I began to feel lightheaded. The tall, gaunt frame of our newest facilities maintenance employee stared back at me. A man I had met only one time. He still wore the work shirt with his name embroidered above the breast pocket, and several days of beard clung to his cheek's hollows. He stood mocking me in some unfathomable, slippery way while I groped for reality. My lightheadedness intensified. My heartbeat whooshed in my ears and sounded so goddamn far away.

He moved when I moved, my motions were his, which made the scene even more surreal. I touched my face, and Alfie touched his, mine, as well. My mind completely rebelled. I didn't even know the questions to ask: didn't know what I didn't know. Finally, Dorothy Parker came to mind: what fresh hell was this?

My knees weakened, my fingers tingled, and my lips numbed. My light headedness degraded into severe tunnel vision. I became nauseated and popped a sweat through skin thick with goosebumps. I reached for my bed to steady myself as Alfie did the same. My knees gave up, and I stupidly remember feeling bad that Alfie was going to pass out too. Then: Why is he in my bedroom?

I woke up on the hardwood of my bedroom floor, one hand propped against the leg of my bed, towel askew, and my entire body freezing cold. I had no memory of passing out.

Nothing felt broken; nothing even hurt too badly. I eased myself upright and looked around. When I saw the mirror, all the sensations and nauseating fear rushed back. The reflection, the faint, the events of the past couple weeks. It was more than I could handle.

My anger, desperation, and frustration boiled over. I opened my dresser and put on the first clothing I saw – a pair of Asics running pants and a t-shirt that said "Hot Springs National Park," and featured a graphic of a deer enjoying a sunset next to a bucolic stream. We had vacationed there when Freddie was 7, and I hadn't worn the t shirt since then.

I jumped in my car and headed toward the school. I had to talk to him, but I didn't know why, and I didn't know what I'd say. How was he involved in all this? What fucking game was my subconscious playing? It was my subconscious. Wasn't it?

We had barely spoken that day. I knew nothing about him other than he was a new custodian: I didn't know his favorite baseball team, or what he did in spare time, what he did before he worked at our school, or hell — even where he was from. But something inside me knew something.

Turning onto 85th street, the street that three blocks further up would dump me into the staff parking lot, I stopped at the first stop sign and nearly passed out again. Impossibly, I saw Alfie Armstrong walking down 85th street toward me as if it were perfectly ok for him to just. . . BE there.

I pulled into a gas station parking lot and lowered my window, shouting as he approached.

He hesitated but gave no sign of recognition.

"Alfie its Mason . . . Dell. From school."

Still nothing, but he began to walk slowly toward my parked car, squinting.

"I teach English. You helped me with some boxes when I was moving into my classroom."

That did it. He finished his approach.

"Ah. Yeah. Hey." He nodded slightly, leaning down to my open window. "Shouldn't you be in . . ."

"Yeah, I called in sick. Look, I really need to talk to you."

"Me?"

I wasn't sure who it made less sense to: him or me. "I know it sounds odd . . ."

"Odd." He took a step backward, untrusting. "At least."

I measured his reluctance. He hadn't run away. Or even walked. I needed to speak with this man for some reason. It was all I could think about after what I'd seen. I just wished I understood why. I gave the moment a beat.

"Listen," I said finally, "I just really need to talk with you. I've had fucked up day, and its barely noon. I need some advice." That felt mildly inaccurate, but I lacked better words.

"Advice about what? I've had a shitty day too."

I briefly reflected on what was the longest sentence he had ever spoken to me. "I'm sorry," I said. "Get in, let me by you a beer and you can tell me about it."

"I barely know you, man. Why would I want to hang out with some guy who grabs me off the street?"

I couldn't argue. But I had an answer, as much as I didn't want to present it this way. "I'm not sure how to answer that. But I need to talk to you . . .because I saw you," I said, and pushed through to the bizarre end. I knew this would either win or lose the moment for me. "In my mirror. Less than an hour ago in my bedroom."

He folded his arms and stared at me. Then it occurred to me.

"Why aren't YOU at the school," I asked, and before he could answer, before the thought was even fully out of my mouth, I knew. "You got fired."

"How the . . ."

"Just get in."

He got in.

DOBY'S PLACE DOWNTOWN NEAR THE LAKE WAS A DRUNK'S BAR. WE PULLED UP in front of the decrepit brick storefront wedged between a pawn shop and a deli. The whole block squatted forgotten in the shadow of a highway overpass.

The recessed door gave way onto a long room with an ancient bar running down one side. Inside, only neon beer signs and grimy plate glass window that covered most of the front wall kept total darkness at bay. The place smelled like old laundry piled in a basement, and a muffled speaker hidden somewhere played old Motorhead, Lemmie Kilmister wailing about the Ace of Spades.

We sat on stools near the back end of the barely-occupied bar.

"Getcha?" Ironically, the bartender looked a lot like Lemmie Kilmister.

"Jameson's. Double," I said. "And his." I threw a thumb toward Alfie "Coke."

The bartender looked at me, then back at Alfie. "Suit yourself." He moved off.

"You sure you don't want a . . ."

"How'd you know I got fired?"

"I . . ."

"It JUST happened. I had the meeting less than a half a fuckn' hour before I saw you."

The bartender set a pint glass of coke in front of Alfie and a highball glass in front of me, into which he poured a generous double whiskey. "Six," he said.

I handed him my credit card. "Keep it open."

He grunted and set my card on the anachronism that served as a cash register. Axl Rose replaced Lemmie on the sound system, and someone racked balls on the pool table. I turned to Alfie.

"I don't know," I said. "I just knew. I knew without knowing."

"That makes no . . ."

"Let me back up."

I related the whole story, starting with the first mirror incident, culminating just an hour earlier, passing out after seeing him in my mirror.

"So, you came to find me," he said after considering my tale for a few moments.

"Yeah, I just thought . . ." I didn't actually know what I thought. "I don't know, maybe seeing you meant something."

"And then it just came to you that I'd gotten fired."

I nodded, shrugged, and finished my whiskey. "What do you think it means? Does it mean anything to you?"

"Fuck if I know." He shifted uncomfortably.

The bartender came by to check on us. He asked if we needed anything by way of raising his eyebrows: a real conversationalist, this one.

I nodded and touched my glass.

"I'll take one too," I assumed Alfie was just reading the room.

The bartender gave us two fresh glasses and poured. I picked mine up and sipped. Alfie slammed the double and grimaced. He put down his glass and for several seconds he sat still, eyes shut tightly, folded into himself, or somewhere in orbit around reality. The bartender looked at me and I shrugged again.

"Another," Alfie said, opening his eyes and nodding.

I raised my glass. "To new friends," I said.

He returned the toast.

Alfie, it turned out, had been fired for lying on his application at the school district. Quite a few years earlier, he had been in a bad spot. He spent way too much time at the bottom of a bottle and ended up owing the wrong kind of people the right amount of money and had no hope of paying it back. The crowd he was into it for wouldn't take kindly to him skipping town, either. They had some leverage on him – he hesitated to say exactly what, other than he was unwilling to pull at that thread.

He learned he could pay back his debt by doing a little extracurricular work and keeping it quiet. Alfie's problem was that he wasn't great at being quiet, especially when he was drinking, which was usually.

One night, at a bar a lot like Doby's, he said, he had one too many – or six or seven too many – and bragged about what he was doing for his newfound friends a little too loudly and in too much detail. While his drinking pals were duly impressed, so were a pair of off-duty police detectives sitting several seats over. Or at least that's what they told him when they picked him up two days later for possession with intent to distribute, possession of a firearm, and a few other gems.

He took a deal and gave up some information on his contact in the organization in exchange for a lighter sentence. With good behavior (he kept his head down and himself to himself in prison) he was out in a couple years, sober and looking for work.

But on his district application, when asked if he had been convicted of a felony, he had said no. Somehow, the administration found out.

I GOT HOME AND MADE A POT OF COFFEE. THE BUZZ FROM THE BAR WAS BIGGER than I realized. I had made the wrong decision driving home. Alfie had elected to walk, saying he needed to clear his head.

Even after hearing Alfie's entire story, I was baffled. Why had I seen him in the mirror? How had I known so certainly that he had gotten fired? Thinking back, I realized I knew it as I drove toward the school looking for him. I never expected to find him in the school. I knew he'd be somewhere outside it. But most of all, why had I needed to hear his story? Why did Alfie's input matter?

The coffee machine beeped its completion, and I poured a cup, leaning in my accustomed spot against the counter. The letter shouted my failure.

I drank the coffee sitting on the couch watching a Friends rerun while sobering up. I decided to shower again before I picked Freddie up from school, so I didn't smell like a bar.

I got as far as the bathroom doorway.

The medicine cabinet stood ajar, the mirror angled toward the door, and I saw myself approach. Then everything melted.

I stood paralyzed. My vision tunneled, leaving only the mirror's center. Like Little Alex in Anthony Burgess's dystopian future, my eyes couldn't block out the atrocities it showed me.

A naked man entered a cave. Was it me? I couldn't tell in the dim underground. Rugged stones cut his bare feet, the ceiling and walls restricted his movement. He pressed on as if pulled by some invisible force. The space shrank by degrees, eventually forcing him to crawl. Each movement flayed his bare flesh against harsh stone until he crawled on bloody knees and palms, moving deeper into the throat of the unknown.

An eerie green light appeared in the distance, and he approached it with anticipation. His back scraped continuously on the impossibly low ceiling, but he progressed until the cave widened, depositing him into the ambient green haze.

He knelt, his bloody knees bearing his weight fully, the tops of his feet and toes scraped raw from the journey, his shoulders and forehead lost blood in rivulets. In the green, he searched. He frantically hunted for something unknown while behind him, a shadow appeared on the wall of the cave, cast by nonexistent illumination, its shoulders portraying a familiar slump, a man defeated.

Back in my bathroom, I shook my head to dislodge the vision. I couldn't take it anymore. Something needed to fucking change, and I didn't know how to make it any better until I met with Dr. Stenson.

I slammed the medicine cabinet and ran to my car, the beginning of a plan in my head.

My watch told me I had an hour until I had to pick Freddie up. It might be enough time to make this happen.

"Dr. Stenson's office." The receptionist picked up on the third ring as I pulled out of my driveway.

"Hi, this is Mason Dell. I called this morning about seeing Dr. Stenson as soon as I could." I swung the car onto 75th street and approached the light at 30th Avenue where I'd make a left. The light was green and I needed to make it.

"Yes Mr. Dell, of course. What can I do for you?"

"Well, I feel like this is an emergency. Today is really bad." I missed the light but took the turn anyway. I challenged the accelerator, flying down the residential street 20 mph above the speed limit. Then I remembered I had been drinking earlier in the day, and backed off the gas.

"I'm sorry you're having such a hard time, Mr. Dell. I wish there was something I could do for you. If you feel like it's an emergency, Dr Stenson would encourage you to call 9-1-1 and get the help you. . ."

"I understand," I said. "Please. I don't want to go to the hospital. I know Dr. Stenson, and she knows me. If I could just talk to her for a few minutes. To, I don't know, start a conversation. THE conversation. I need to get this out, and she knows me." I realized I had said that already. But I sacrificed my word choice to desperation.

"Dr. Stenson is going out of town Wednesday and will be gone. . ."

"What about tomorrow?"

"She doesn't have any openings I'm afraid . . . "

"Look, I know you're only doing your job," I caught a bit of good luck, and turned right onto 80th street just as the light turned yellow, then merged smoothly into the left turn lane. My destination was just ahead. An outlier in a large strip mall's parking lot. "I have hallucinated twice in the past 6 hours, and I don't mean just seeing tracers. I'm seeing people. Whole scenarios playing out, that I KNOW are not there."

"That's really between you and the doctor," she said.

I turned left into the shopping center's parking lot maze, and then right into the parking lot of the Dollar Tree, guiding my car to the first open spot I saw. Screeching to a halt, I threw the car in park. "Please."

She paused, sighed, and then said not unkindly, "Can I put you on hold for a minute?"

"Yes. Please do," I was thrilled with anything other than a "no."

Seconds stretched as I sat and listened to The Girl From Ipanema by someone other than Getz and Gilberto. Mercifully, eventually, she came back on the line.

"Dr. Stenson says she can squeeze you in tomorrow afternoon about two. It'll be a shorter than normal appointment, but I'm afraid it's all we can do, Mr. Dell.

"Fine. Perfect. Thank you so much. I appreciate it more than you know."

"You're welcome. We will see you tomorrow."

I got out of my car and started walking toward the store to buy supplies for the second half of my plan, while it solidified itself in my head. "Two. Thanks again." I hung up and opened the door, glancing at my watch. I really needed to hustle.

BACK AT HOME, SHOPPING BAG IN HAND, I WALKED TO THE BATHROOM. I HAD to pick Freddie up in 20 minutes, but not before doing something. I forced calm on myself, or as close as I could approximate it. The front of the construction paper package showed a friendly cat someone had made from cutting shapes out of all the colors of paper in the package. I also fished out the fresh roll of masking tape. Ripping them both open – it almost felt like a shame to rip through the picture of the cat – I set to work.

I used four sheets of paper to cover my bathroom mirror. I chose the darker colors: black, brown, dark purple, dark green. Their opacity allowed me to use only one layer. I closed the cabinet and found that I couldn't see myself at all.

I went to my bedroom and repeated the process with the full-length mirror where I had seen Alfie Armstrong that morning. That one took me eight sheets.

Satisfied with my removal of the primary offenders, I moved throughout the house, finishing up the package, covering everything that threw my reflection back at me. I covered the television in the living room, the kitchen sliding glass doors (16 pieces of paper) and the window above the hall tree, among other potential offenders, Then I walked back to my bedroom.

I approached the window parallel to the wall, so I couldn't see my reflection until I was directly in front of it.

It reflected my bed, and most of the room for that matter, but not now, not that current moment. It showed me my wife and I. The two of us sat in bed, young enough that it had to be pre-Freddie. She read a magazine, and I tapped away at my laptop.

I stared. I hadn't seen her move, live, other than the few videos on my phone, in years.

Her presence was disarming. My heart battered the inside of my ribcage. I whirled to the bed and of course, found it empty. The bedroom mirror offered no help: I had covered it. When I returned my eyes to the window, the scene was gone. I saw only myself, still dressed in sweats and an old t-shirt, with a mostly-empty construction paper package in one hand and a used-up roll of masking tape in the other. My fingers numbed and lost their grip on both. I lowered myself to the floor and sobbed frustration and grief into my hands.

I WAS NEARLY LATE TO PICK FREDDIE UP AT SCHOOL. HE SAT AT THE END OF the bus lane when I got there, and I felt sad seeing him alone. Inspired at the time (and feeling no small amount of guilt) I asked if he wanted to get ice cream on the way home. He responded that he was 14, not four, and he had homework to do.

"What . . .is with all the construction paper?" He asked as he walked into the kitchen from the back hallway.

"Oh," I walked into the kitchen. In my desperation to rid my house of reflections, I hadn't thought about the potential for questions.

"Seriously dad. What is it? What's going on? First the toothbrush, then Luigi's, now this. You think I'm just a kid. That I don't notice. But I see things. You're scaring me." He dropped his backpack on the kitchen floor with a gravitational thud.

"It's part of an assignment I'm thinking about doing with my senior seminar students." School was almost always a good excuse for odd behavior. I had learned that through the years.

"An assignment." It was a statement. His expression gave my words the lie.

"Yes. A poetry assignment." I shrugged and chuckled. "It's a long story. And I'm not even sure about it. I'm trying it out myself first."

Freddie stared at me for a long moment while I twisted my fingers.

He shook his head. "Whatever it is, covering it up won't make it go away." He hoisted his backpack and walked down the hallway.

There was no doubt in my mind that Freddie was right.

I heard his bedroom door slam just before I picked up the phone to call Dominoes. I was in no mood to cook.

I WOKE UP ON THE COUCH HOURS LATER, SURE I HAD HEARD SOMETHING. HAD I been dreaming? What had it been about? And what was that fucking pounding noise?

I realized the pounding was my front door when I heard it again. I looked at my coffee table, half covered in beer cans. That's what had happened. I fought my fog, my hearing and vision still filmed by the haze created when alcohol and sleep conspire.

The pounding again: this time louder.

I looked at my watch: 2:30 am. What the fuck could possibly be happening? I swung my feet around and stumbled, catching myself before I hit the floor. Eventually I made it down the hallway.

Alfie Armstrong stood on my front stoop. He wore the same pants and work shirt as when I'd seen him earlier, but with a faded denim jacket over the top. His hair looked entirely forgotten and he smelled like a distillery tour I once took.

I stood half in and half out of my house, holding the screen door open. "Alfie, what are you . . ."

"Here." He thrust a three-quarters empty Southern Comfort bottle at me.

"What is this?" I asked, not sure about any of it.

"A fucking mistake." He took a half step toward me and shoved the bottle into my chest. Knocking me slightly backward.

I instinctively clasped it.

"My mistake but your damn fault. Seven years sober before today." He stepped backward, nearly falling off the stoop's ledge onto the sidewalk. "Seven damn years. Then you had to drag me to a bar. I hadn't set foot in one 'cause I knew what would happen."

"I didn't know. I just . . ."

"Never mind you just. I walked home to clear my head. But it wasn't. Clear. Not anywhere close." He climbed unsteadily back onto the stoop. He grabbed the bottle back and shook it. "I stopped halfway there and bought this." He shook it again for emphasis in case I wasn't' clear on what he meant. "And I couldn't wait to get home to drink it."

Alfie began to tear up and dropped his arm to his side. I stepped fully out of my house and let the screen door close.

"I was changed, man," he said. I was a better person. A person. Not some puppet controlled by THIS." He held the bottle back up at eye level. "I was the REAL me."

He apparently expected me to say something.

"I'm sorry. I didn't . . . ."

"Yeah, well, that ain't good enough. And, you know what?" He paused and I waited. "I didn't believe your stupid mirror bullshit anyway. You need help man. You need to see a shrink."

This time, the pause was much longer.

"I know." It sucked to admit. "I have an appointment tomorrow. I just thought since I had seen you, and that if I could talk to you about it . . . I don't know."

"I didn't believe you." He continued as if I hadn't said anything at all. "But I got so fuckin' drunk after we talked and after drinking this much more that it happened to me too. I looked in the damn mirror and I wasn't moving right."

I shook my head, sure I had heard him wrong. "What? It happened to you too?"

"Yeah. The whole world's spinnin' a little bit." I could see that was true. "And I looked in the mirror and when I looked left, he took a minute to catch up. And when I walked away, he FOL-lowed me. Not when I walked. Later. Motherfucker didn't even look like me. Looked like some strung out dude I didn't recognize."

Alfie chose that moment to vomit into the hedges that flanked my front stoop. It was a long, low, gurgling sound and I was instantly nauseated. He emptied the contents of his stomach in several heaves and continued to dry heave for a minute afterward. I was glad it was dark and that my porch light wasn't on.

Oblivious to the vomiting, he continued. "That's how drunk I am. First, I thought it actually happened, like you said. That it was real. But I realized it was just you. Just your story and the booze. You put that shit in my head and the booze made me see it. So, you know what, fuck you, and fuck this shit."

He unscrewed the bottle cap and dumped the rest over the top of where he puked.

"No more," he said. "No more of this shit. I kicked it once and I'll kick it again. I want to be the REAL me again. Not drunk all the goddamn time. And no more of you, either. I don't know what's all fucked up in your brain, but I don't want any part of it. So good luck."

He turned his back on me and stumbled down the step onto the sidewalk. The stumble caused him to drop the bottle, and it clinked to the sidewalk. He bent and retrieved it, then tossed it to me underhand.

"Here ya go." I caught it just before it landed at my feet. "A souvenir from our day of friendship. Have a good one."

He walked down the block out of site, and I never saw Alfie Armstrong again.

I took the bottle inside and set it on the counter, next to the coffee maker which I didn't bother setting up for the morning. Sleep was evasive.

I JOLTED AWAKE TO THE ROAR OF CRUNCHY GUITARS. MY PULSE SLAMMED through my skull causing a visual beat and audible thudding, momentarily burying the sound of the power chords. After a few deep breaths, the music resurfaced. I glanced at my clock. Five thirty a.m. – The wave of sound had, ironically, crashed at just the right moment.

"Alexa, stop!" Dag Nasty again. Twice in just a few days. That felt a little too coincidental. I rubbed my temples to slow my heartbeat.

Invasively, the events of last night resurfaced in my consciousness. I regretted causing Alfie all the trouble, and my stomach clenched recalling him vomiting. But that – all of it - was a horse long gone.

I walked slowly to the kitchen where I found Alfie's SoCo bottle in the sink. I tossed it into the trash and loaded grounds into Mr. Coffee's waiting maw. My head felt less than correctly screwed on and I needed my first cup of Joe to straighten me out.

While the coffee brewed, I leaned in my accustomed place. I took the letter off the refrigerator to reread it. Halfway through, it dropped to the floor through instantly weak fingers.

The bottle. Had been in the sink.

I inched to the garbage can and lifted the bottle out, examining it at arm's length like roadkill or an alien artifact. I spun it slowly as if there were an answer somewhere on, or in it but I didn't find anything other than my own distorted reflection.

Alfie had thought there was an answer in it. Somewhere at the bottom he thought he'd find out why he had gotten fired. Well, he knew why he had gotten fired. But I guess he thought he would find a way to deal with getting fired. Instead, he fell off the wagon and found a stranger in the mirror. Like I had.

A stranger in the mirror.

The air in the kitchen froze. The only sound was the guttural gurgle and drip from Mr. Coffee, and it all sounded distorted. The moment bulged, bloated in my mind with meaning, pregnant with a realization that wouldn't be born. It was an itch between the shoulder blades, and my goddamn arms were in slings.

I tightened my grip on the bottle neck and turned it again, distorting my face in the bottle's contours. Each angle showed a different me. Each corner jumped at me, and I stared back.

How would I find what I was looking for?

Mr. Coffee gurgled its last. The thought clicked.

Fuck.

"Alexa, play Million Days by Dag Nasty."

"Million Days by Dag Nasty on Amazon Music." She was always so cooperative. In the instant before Dale Nixon's guitar slammed into me again, I saw the dots: the bottle, the letter, the mirror, the song. Now I needed the lines.

Ten seconds of visceral power chords shot through me before Colin Sears's drums gave it structure. First disjoined and syncopated, he punished the toms. Ten more seconds in, and the guitars had shocked it into a bass-snare heartbeat and the whole thing roared ahead. Dots all. Then came the lines. The web strands I'd been missing.

> *look in the mirror*
> *who's staring at me*
> *reflections showing everything but the pain that's underneath*
> *I turn around and walk away but the images stay in my mind*
> *wish I could see things clearly*
> *wish I could see through all this doubt*
> *and if I had a million days*
> *would I find what I'm looking for?*
> *who I'm looking for?*
> *if I had a million days...*

I reread the letter as the song pressed on. The stupid letter that had pounded me into submission had convinced me to stop writing, to stop pursuing something I always loved, to stop being me. The real me.

I CHUCKLED. I COULDN'T HELP IT. STARING AT THE GODDAMN LETTER IN ONE hand and an empty bottle of Southern Comfort in the other: realization, then understanding, then unbridled laughter. I laughed until my cheeks cramped. I doubled over and leaned against the kitchen cabinets. Tears streamed down my cheeks. I lost control of my fingers and dropped letter and then the bottle, which clunked to the kitchen hardwood and bounced once. The letter was MY bottle of SoCo.

I continued laughing.

I slid down the cabinets until I sat on the floor, legs straight out in front of me, eyes brimming with tears. I shuddered out a deep breath, calming the spasms. I wiped my eyes with the back of my hands.

"Dad?" Freddie's voice, hesitantly from the hallway, nearly drowned out by the solo. I hadn't heard his bedroom door open.

"Alexa! Stop! Yeah. I'm here. In the kitchen."

The soft sound of bare feet.

"Where? I don't see . . ."

"Down here, on the floor."

He walked around the side of the counter where I sat. "What are you doing?" Sheet tattoos covered his cheeks, and his heavy-lidded eyes sought focus. But somehow, concern cut through the layers of sleep and hesitant voice.

I looked up at him and started to laugh again but it stuck in my throat. "I'm sorry." He was young, but he was no dummy.

He slid down next to me on the floor and rubbed his eyes. "I'm worried about you, Dad. Things have been weird again."

"I've been stressed with the school year starting and everything. I'm ok."

"It's more than that." Kids are intuitive, but I knew there was understanding buttressing his insight. His gaze found the letter and the whiskey bottle. Then he looked back at me. The question was plain.

"I wasn't drinking this early, don't worry." I said, picking up the bottle. "This was . . . well a friend left it here."

"Who?"

"No one you know. He stopped by late last night. After you went to bed." I watched him watch me. I watched his decision to believe what I was saying about the whiskey. "You're right, though, Fred. It's more than just school stress. It's something I've been doing wrong for a while. But I figured it out. And it's all over."

"Are you sure?"

"Yeah." I nodded looking at the letter, still clutched in my hand. "I'm very sure."

"I've read that letter, you know." He abruptly zagged when I was still dealing with his zig. Of course he had read it. It had hung on the refrigerator for months. Why hadn't I thought of him reading it too? "Why did you keep it for so long? Is that what this is about?"

Good questions. Did I have the right answers? I was pretty sure I did: It had made sense at the time. It was a reminder of what someone told me were my limitations. A reminder of how to NOT feel like a failure anymore. A reminder I had taken at face value. And my belief in that had caused all of this.

"It felt important at the time, like something I wanted to remember." I didn't know how to justify it. At that moment, after all that had happened, it didn't make sense. but I wasn't going to lie to him. "I don't think I do anymore."

"You wrote a lot after mom died." He rubbed his eyes again and straightened his t shirt. Why'd you stop? You said you liked it. Things felt normal to me then, too."

The air between us felt calm for the first time in months. The communication wide open.

"I don't know, man," I said, but obviously I did. "Probably because of this." I waved the letter.

"Why do you care what that guy who wrote that thinks? It's just his opinion, right?"

I guess I really had raised him right.

"Absolutely," I said.

"You should try again. Maybe it would help."

I had never been more proud. He had figured it out so much faster than me.

"I'm sure you're exactly right." I ruffled his hair and we both stood up. When had he gotten taller than me? "Go get ready for school."

He shuffled down the hallway toward his bedroom. I cringed when his door slammed. He always slammed the goddamn door.

I threw the empty whisky bottle away. It landed with a fsshunk as its weight pulled the garbage bag tight.

Then I read the letter one last time. Freddie's words continued to resonate. When had my son become my teacher?

I ripped it into pieces and held my hand above the garbage can. With what felt like theatrical deliberation, I released them and watched them flutter downward. They drifted hesitantly toward the trash, snowflakes on a lazy breeze. And then they disappeared.

I headed toward the bathroom to shower and shave. As I passed my desk in the living room I stopped and fished out a blank legal pad and my favorite Zebra pen. I plopped the pad in the middle of the desk and wrote on the first line:

Mirror story: What happens when a man's reflection doesn't match his actions?

I tapped the pen against my teeth and nodded. It was a step in the right direction.

Then I walked the rest of the way through the house, tearing down construction paper as I went.

End

ABOUT THE AUTHOR

Dale Alexander is a writer from Southeast Wisconsin, USA.

BY DARRYLE PURCELL

After 32 years of marriage, I believed Dottie and I were due a celebration in Paradise.

The kids were grown and gone from the nest and our world had become a daily grind with no goals. The lack of children in the house had left our home as silent as a Douglas Fairbanks' pirate movie without a piano. My job at the dealership was going nowhere and Dottie's work as an elementary school library clerk had ended due to budget cuts. Life in Hesperia, California, had lost its glamour.

I had a little more than four hundred bucks squirreled away that I had planned on using for a new Smith and Wesson handgun, but I decided our marriage could use something else; something that might make it less likely that I would use a gun on myself. Dottie and I needed to get away from our current existence for a week's vacation.

"That Pat Sajak is a real card," Dottie said while watching her favorite game show. She was seated on the couch with a TV tray in front of her holding a plate of pizza and a wine glass. The bottle of merlot was next to her feet. "Wouldn't you just love to spin that wheel?"

I grunted from the kitchen table where I was cleaning my Luger. One can never be too prepared, I always say to just about anyone who is unfortunate enough to get into a conversation with me. Obviously, I'm not the friendliest guy in town – for good reasons. I've learned that people are all out to take advantage of the other guy. Oh, I smile and slap backs and compliment customers as I sell them pre-owned vehicles that may or may not continue running long enough for their checks to clear. But I know every one of them would kick in the door of my manufactured home and rob me blind, if they could.

"Look at that! It's just like the one on Pat's show!" Dottie squealed as a commercial pimped Las Vegas as the destination for fun. A huge gambling wheel spun leading into images of beautiful couples laughing as colorful slot machines poured coins into their laps. Then a montage appeared of top entertainers like Travis Tritt, Willie Nelson, Donny Osmond and Barry Manilow, strutting across stages and hugging middle-aged women.

My mind joined the wheel in spinning as I felt like the answer to all of our needs was being placed in front of me. Dottie and I needed a vacation and, at that moment, Las Vegas looked like Paradise. A week in Sin City would do wonders for us, I thought. But just how far would $400 take us? I sighed and pondered the situation. What we needed was a smaller, less-expensive Las Vegas – a Paradise Lite.

I put my Luger away and got on the computer. I figured I might be able to afford to vacation in either Mesquite or Laughlin, Nevada, both of which were much-smaller version of Las Vegas. They had the basics of a Vegas experience – casinos, entertainment and cheap dining.

I was amazed that Laughlin had the best prices, even though Mesquite was farther away and smaller. I could get a week in Laughlin at a casino overlooking the Colorado River for $15 per day with free buffet luncheons and a pre-paid card for $100 in slot play. As I booked our room I felt giddy knowing that I was about to revive our marriage not unlike Dr. Frankenstein throwing the switch to bring lightning-life to his creation.

Then the hard part – I had to keep my mouth shut for the rest of the week. I didn't want to spoil Dottie's surprise and I had to arrange vacation time from the dealership. Big Red agreed to fill in for me at the lot, which was no skin off his nose in that any sales would just be more money in his pocket.

THURSDAY EVENING I WENT OUT TO THE BACKYARD STORAGE SHED AND FOUND what I needed for the trip. In a box, I had some of my favorite 1970s colorful polyester shirts, which I could still wear. Maybe fortunately, my bell-bottoms were too tight. I did my packing in secret. And although my comb-over was getting pretty thin, I used those few days to lengthen my sideburns.

Finally the end of the week arrived. It was time to spring my surprise. I walked around in front of the couch where Dottie was watching television.

"Buy a vowel!" she screamed. "Lance. What are you doing? I'm watching that."

"We're going on vacation," I said. "We're leaving tomorrow morning and will be spending a week in beautiful Laughlin, Nevada."

I watched her face. She was silent for a moment. Looking down, I noticed her lap was damp. She had either spilled her wine or wet herself. I didn't know if it was because she was excited or just a coincidence, but hoped it was the former.

"But, how can we afford…?"

"We have the money. I've booked the room. It's only a two-hour drive and we will be in Paradise."

"But…."

It wasn't the reaction I was hoping for, but I figured she would be thrilled once we arrived at our resort hotel.

IT WAS ALMOST NOON WHEN WE DROVE INTO LAUGHLIN. THE STRIP IS FAIRLY short and made up of a variety of unique architecture, basically large buildings to house gamblers. Our resort hotel was designed to look like a flying saucer that had crashed into the Colorado River. We parked our own vehicle to avoid paying a tip to a valet parking attendant wearing a futuristic, green-alien suit. Our car thermometer told us it was 114 degrees outside and I wondered how someone could wear such an outfit and work in direct sunlight.

"Pretty hot work," I said as I passed the valet attendant, who seemed to be about 17 years old.

"It's not bad," he said. "Wait until it gets hot."

We carried our bags into the lobby, checked in and went looking for our room. Apparently, there wasn't any way to get to anywhere without going through the casino. Large, colorful, loud slot machines were everywhere as we worked our way through the crowded aisles. I didn't see any of the beautiful people from the Las Vegas television commercial but, after looking around, I felt like I was younger than I thought. There were a lot of wheelchairs and oxygen tanks and the air had an over-powering essence of cigarette smoke and wet Depends.

Our room on the sixth floor was small and seemed to be designed with just enough comfort to send its occupants down to the casino floor. There was a bed, a chair and a small chest of drawers with a television on it. The window did have a great view of the river.

Dottie turned on the television, which was obviously local cable. Out of 45 (not pay-per-view) stations, 44 specialized in infomercials. But wait! There's more! One local cable channel offered a version of local news that would have been made fun of by the residents of Mayberry, followed by scheduled programming of old (public domain) television shows. I noticed in the guide provided with our room that in the evening's episode of Martin Kane, Private Eye, William Gargan was to deal with his most challenging murder case. The resort sure made it inviting to leave the room and enter the casino.

I put on my best polyester flowered shirt with the giant peace sign and a red newsboy cap to cover my comb-over. As I left to go downstairs, Dottie was still checking the guide to see if Wheel of Fortune was offered on any of the channels. She said she might join me later.

My first priority was to check the whole place out. The cocktail waitresses wore a delightful version of the green alien outfits with net stockings, antennae in their hair and fuzzy bras. Each room had a different extraterrestrial name. The casino where I was standing was called the Uranus Room. In the far corner was a stage and small dance floor. A sign showed three young men with instruments and stated that they were going to perform a Tribute to Dino, Desi and Billy at 8 p.m.

WINDING MY WAY THROUGH THE CROWD AND THE ESSENCE I MENTIONED EARLIER, I found an exit that led to the famous Laughlin River Walk. There I found fresh air and the beautiful blue Colorado River. The walkway linked most of the casinos along the river. As I strolled past the next-door gaming establishment I smiled at everyone I saw coming the other way. Very few smiled back. I thought about it later and figured it was because I hadn't started gambling yet and they had.

It looked to be what Ed Sullivan used to call "a really big show" week in Laughlin in that the neighbor casino had a large lighted marquee advertising a reunion concert of the Cowsills while the next one touted a mixing of classic musical entertainers with Blood, Sweat and one of the dogs from Three Dog Night. I wondered if Tears had passed on.

On my way back, I marveled at the style of our casino resort. The building looked just like one of those 1950s, Ray Harryhausen-style UFOs sticking up out of the ground. The hotel rooms were in a tower that connected to the saucer-casino. As I paused to watch two skunks engaging in lewd behavior along the river below the walkway, I heard a scream. Turning quickly, I saw a flash of something red falling. A human being hit the ground with a loud crunching splat not 10 feet from me.

The victim had been a middle-aged woman wearing a now-stained red dress. Her feet were bare and it looked like one of her sleeves had been torn almost off. I looked closely to see her hand was clutching a yellow newsboy cap somewhat like the one I had just pushed back from my forehead.

Three elderly ladies wearing Women's Army Corps reunion shirts stood next to me with shocked looks on their faces. A blind man and his service dog were near the railing that kept people from falling into the river. The dog barked at him several times, yet he continued to ask, "What?" I think he might have been deaf as well.

A very upset man wearing a plaid sweater came through the door and stopped suddenly at the sight of the body. He held his hand up to his mouth. He was balder than I was, and his attempt at a comb-over was blowing the wrong way.

Within seconds, men wearing yellow T-shirts with "Security" stenciled on them took control of the area and started moving everyone away from the body. Another crew of people rushed out of the casino with a stretcher and a blanket. They began to pick up the victim and move her.

"Hold on," I yelled. "The police are going to want to see that."

"We work with the police," one very large security man said. "We saw the situation and now we need to remove the victim and clean the mess. I'll deal with the police as soon as they get here."

The body was removed in the time it took for him to tell me that. Next, two women showed up with mops, buckets and cans of spray cleaner. Within minutes, it just looked like someone had spilled a couple of beers on the sidewalk.

"Musta lost her shirt on the crap tables," a woman in an electric wheelchair said to me. "Some folks don't know how to gamble. They come here thinking they're gonna get rich and they lose everything they have."

"You mean you think that was a suicide?" I said.

"She's not the first to take a long leap into this sidewalk," she said. "She's not even the first this month."

She then lit a cigarette and rolled off toward the next gaming establishment, her wheels going through the newly washed area and leaving wet tire tracks. I turned and went back into the casino. The slot machines were still clanging; poker and blackjack players were concentrating with dead expressions in the pit; dice were still rolling. I needed a drink.

I PULLED UP A STOOL AT THE URANUS MOON BAR AND ORDERED A RUM AND Coke. The bartender was wearing a traditional black vest, white shirt and bowtie along with a pair of house antennae.

"When do you think the police will arrive?" I asked.

"What for?"

"To investigate the death of that lady who hit the cement a couple of minutes ago."

"You saw that?" he asked.

"Yep."

"Well, I wouldn't say anything if I were you," he said. "It doesn't help business for people to spread stories about suicides at a casino. And, as for the police, they will take statements from our security people and help keep it quiet as far as the press is concerned."

"How can they decide it was a suicide without an investigation?"

"They always do," he said. "Now it would be a good idea to just forget about it. Those security guys are touchy. They don't like rumors being spread and they are the law around here."

I lit up a cigar and thought about that. I decided to forget about the incident as I valued my kneecaps.

"I'll have a large glass of red ale," said the bald man in the plaid sweater at the other end of the bar. He seemed much more relaxed than he was when I saw him earlier.

He took his mug of ale and turned on his barstool to face out at the casino action. He had a big smile on his face. Licking his right hand, he smoothed his comb-over toward the other side of his head. Then he reached into his pocket, pulled out the yellow newsboy cap that I had last seen clutched in the hand of the corpse and put it over his shiny head.

My eyes got larger as I began to understand the significance. He was the victim's husband. I stood up and walked over to him. He sat calmly as I handed him a cigar.

"You've earned this," I said, while noticing the three fingernail scratches on the left side of his neck.

Then, as I turned and walked away, he began flirting with one of the alien cocktail waitresses.

My $100 pre-paid slot-play card was still in my pocket, unused, when I returned to our room. Dottie was sitting in a very uncomfortable-looking chair in front of the television. She had a big glass of wine in her hand and a pizza in her lap that she had obviously ordered through room service.

"Buy a vowel!" she yelled. "Oh, hi, Lance. I found a channel with my show."

I looked at her and thought a moment. Then I checked out the window, opened it, and smiled.

The End

ABOUT THE AUTHOR

Darryle Purcell has had a variety of jobs during his lifetime — including soldier, illustrator, editorial cartoonist, newspaper managing editor and government flack.

He served in the Army as an infantry paratrooper in the First Cavalry Division in Vietnam (1965-66) and then stateside as a medic, first in the 101st Airborne Division, then in the 82nd Airborne Division. Following the military, he worked his way through college, graduating with an art degree from Cal State University Long Beach, which led to a career as a cartoonist in magazines, newspapers, educational comic books and Saturday morning animated television shows.

Purcell's political cartoons garnered quite a few awards in California during the 1980s and early '90s, while his work as a daily newspaper managing editor in the '90s and first few years of the new century led to many statewide awards in Arizona for news and feature columns and editorials. From 2005 through 2012, he was a public information director for a county in Arizona.

Purcell currently writes and illustrates the *Hollywood Cowboy Detectives*, *Man of the Mist*, *Ghost Squad*, *Geezers* and *Vermin* pulp adventures from his home in rural Arizona, where he lives with his wife Patricia.

$2 DOWN
BRAND NEW
CORONA GENUINE Model #3
Lowest Price — Easiest Terms Ever Offered
HERE's your chance to own that brand new Genuine Model 3 Corona you've wanted — on the easiest terms ever offered — at LOWEST PRICE ever offered. Complete in every detail: back spacer, etc. Manufacturer's Guarantee. Recognized the world over as the finest, strongest, sturdiest portable built.
Yours for 10 DAYS FREE

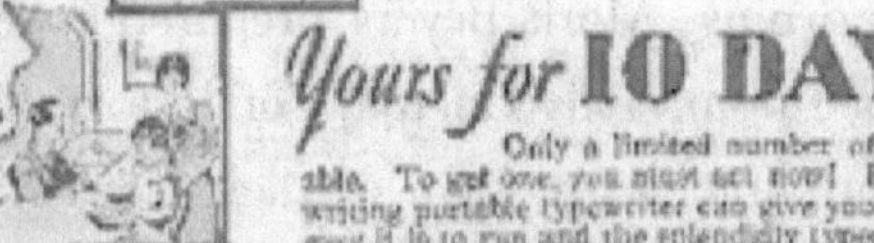

Carrying Case FREE
If You Act Now!
Save Money — Use this Coupon

IN THE MIND OF THE BEHOLDER

BY MURRAY EILAND

The air buzzed with drones delivering packages, and self-driving cars zipped silently along smart roads. Sleek, nearly invisible wires tethered people to their electronic devices.

On a crisp autumn morning, Mark Beyers prepared to enter the Rare Book and Manuscript Room. This sanctuary of history, filled with irreplaceable documents, prohibited any form of digital duplication for fear that something found here could cause problems related to the old world—Earth. Few were granted unrestricted access to this sanctum, and Mark's familiar presence went unquestioned. He disconnected his wire from his phone, feeling momentarily adrift without his link to the digital world.

Inside the room, Mark lost himself in the delicate pages of an ancient manuscript. Despite having sifted through these old texts before, some of the information found within still staggered the mind. On the old world, for instance, traditional marriages were portrayed as joyous occasions, celebrated with grand ceremonies that symbolized deep commitments between individuals. The joining of two souls had once been a universal right cherished by families and communities alike. The regime imposed no restrictions; love had been free to flourish without the interference of bureaucratic command and control.

Marriage had become a privilege, a contractual bond available only to those who met the regime's rigid criteria. Compatibility was calculated by algorithms, not hearts. Genetic markers, socioeconomic projections, and psychological profiles were weighed and approved— or denied— by Utopia's omnipresent AI overseer, the Arbiter. Love, as it had once been understood, was an inefficiency in this brave new order. The ancient, idealized union described in dusty, contraband books now seemed almost comical, a relic of a world untethered from reason. Mark couldn't help but ponder the implications. Was this truly progress, or merely another chain dressed as salvation? Not that it mattered; questions like these were dangerous to voice.

The Arbiter's dictum echoed in his mind like a mantra: 'Society must evolve. Evolution demands sacrifice.' Mark knew better than to linger on these thoughts, but it was hard not to, considering these like-sounding phrases were plastered on posters all over the University. Free will was an illusion; his generation's needs and desires were preordained by a regime that saw everything, calculated everything, controlled everything.

Even meat, something as primal and universal as the human craving for flesh, had been excised from the cultural palate. Once, it had been a cornerstone of life, its aroma wafting through bustling steakhouses and roadside diners, its sizzle punctuating gatherings of families and friends. Now, that world was as foreign as the idea of privacy.

Mark ran a finger along the cracked leather spine of a smuggled pre-Utopian cookbook, the faded title spelling out The Carnivore's Guide. It was a relic of the Before—a time when humans had slaughtered animals en masse, and yet … they had celebrated it. The pages detailed recipes as though the killing was merely another step in a cherished tradition. He felt a tinge of revulsion and fascination as he skimmed instructions for roasting, searing, and grilling various animals.

Could they really have lived this way?

He came across a picture titled, "double bacon cheeseburger," and something in the back of his mind told his tastebuds to water.

"Stop staring at that." A woman's voice startled him.

"Whoa! Hey, I wasn't doing anything—" Mark immediately came off sounding guilty.

"You really shouldn't be digging through this stuff without proper clearance."

Mark's eyes darted to the walls, their faux-marble surface concealing a labyrinth of sensors and audio monitors.

Naomi nodded. "Just…be cool, okay. You don't know who's listening."

Mark carefully closed the book and tucked it back into the hollowed-out cavity beneath the floorboards. "It's just a book."

"Sure. To you and me, maybe, but to other, more important people, it's never just a book. Trust me, I learned the hard way."

"The hard way?"

"The Arbiter has been recalibrating surveillance thresholds. They're targeting subversive interests. Anything nostalgic for the Before—"

"Becomes treason," Mark finished for her.

"Ah! So you do pay attention to current events."

The regime's official stance on the eradication of meat was one of morality, so it was no wonder this book was hidden away. Slaughterhouses were barbaric, their existence a stain on humanity's ethical progress. Or so they were told. Reality, Mark suspected, was far more insidious. The state-controlled nutrient paste dispensed to every citizen at prescribed intervals wasn't just a replacement for meat; it was a tool. Engineered for maximum efficiency, it dulled hunger, muted cravings, and perhaps— though no one dared confirm it— stifled rebellious thoughts— nothing more.

Still, Mark couldn't suppress the gnawing doubt.

Were people truly repulsed by slaughterhouses, or had the Arbiter programmed them to be remembered that way?

"It's strange, isn't it?" Mark murmured, glancing at Naomi. "That something so fundamental— so human—could just… disappear."

Her expression hardened. "It didn't disappear. It was erased. And if we talk any louder, we might just disappear, too. Let's head out to the waiting area; there are less ears out there."

Outside the window of the waiting area, the city of Utopia stretched in every direction, a gleaming labyrinth of glass and steel. From the towering spires of the Central Authority to the monotonous rows of residential units, everything was pristine, efficient, and utterly devoid of soul. The only sounds were the hum of drones patrolling the sky and the faint, rhythmic beeping of surveillance nodes scanning the streets below.

Mark's gaze fell on a billboard projecting a rotating image of a smiling couple with the caption: 'Happiness Through Harmony: Let the Arbiter Guide You.' Beneath the saccharine slogan was a scrolling ticker of citizen metrics— birth rates, productivity indices, crime suppression statistics.

"Really hate to split, but I have to get going," Naomi said, latching the door behind her.

"But I thought you said—"

"Look, Mark— just stay out of there, okay?"

And that was that. The woman Mark barely remembered offered him a nervous smile as she hesitantly stepped away from the Book and Manuscript Room before finally disappearing down the hall.

Once he was certain she was gone, Mark quietly ducked back inside and continued searching the old records.

Time slipped away unnoticed until the hands of the old-style clock were nearing the end of the day. As Mark stepped back out into the hallway, a wave of vertigo hit him. The familiar corridors of the University felt both recognizable and alien at the same time.

"Did I stand up too fast?" he wondered. His balance faltered, and he propped himself up against the wall with his hand. "What is going on?"

He stumbled outside and found the campus transformed. The architecture remained the same, but subtle differences in design and signage created a sense of dissonance. Students wore unfamiliar styles of clothing, their devices sporting interfaces he'd never seen before. Even the language they spoke, though English, carried a peculiar accent and strange idioms.

Mark placed the back of his hand against his forehead to check himself for a fever, but it felt cool to the touch. The dizziness began to fade, replaced by nausea.

Dazed, Mark reached into his side pocket and grabbed his phone. His hands shook as he hurriedly reconnected his wire. His fingers trembled as he dialed Julie, his girlfriend and fellow PhD student. The phone rang and rang. Mark continued to scan his surroundings, noticing more bizarre anomalies.

"Hey!" Julie answered, her voice warm and familiar. Hearing it sent a wave of calm over Mark, but only for a moment.

"Julie? It's Mark. Something—something's happened! I don't know where I am. Everything's different; I can't explain it."

"Whoa, hey, calm down, babe."

"Julie, I'm freaking out here. It's like I wandered into the Twilight Zone or something."

She took a moment to respond. "Wait, are you serious?"

"Yes!"

"Okay, hold on! Where are you?" she asked, growing more concerned.

"Can you come to the Rare Book Room?"

"Of course. Stay where you are, Mark. I'm on my way."

As Mark waited, the reality of his situation began to sink in. It was a long shot and utterly unfathomable, but somehow, he had managed to cross into a parallel world—one where everything was both eerily familiar and profoundly different. His historian's mind raced with questions and possibilities. Why did this happen? Or better yet, how did this happen?

At first glance, people looked the same—two eyes, two ears, a nose, a mouth—all of that checked out, but the environment was altered. Mark's heart raced as he stepped onto the University campus. The placards on the buildings were different. The statue of the campus founder had been replaced by someone else—a woman Mark didn't recognize. He crouched to examine the bronze plate at the base of the statue, which proclaimed this woman to be the founder of the University. His hand trembled as he pulled up his phone, the glow of its screen a small, comforting tether to familiarity. Frantically, he began to search, his fingers tapping out queries as he tried to find answers—anything that would help him make sense of this disorienting reality. Significant buildings, he thought, that's a good place to start. Like a texting-obsessed teenager, he hammered one location after another, searching for landmarks or notable sites he knew—but nothing.

It didn't take long for the grim realization to set in: all of history, as he knew it, was now different. His breath caught as he scrolled through pages of search results, each one confirming the vast discrepancies between this world and the one he had left behind.

His mind spiraled with disbelief. How could history itself be rewritten? The implications were staggering, shaking the very foundation of his understanding of the world. His hands were clammy, and his chest tightened as he grappled with the enormity of what he had discovered.

"Hey?" A hand landed on his shoulder, jolting him from his thoughts.

"Whoa!" He dropped his phone, but luckily, it didn't break.

"Babe, are you good?" Julie asked.

Mark was as white as a ghost. His heart pounded in his chest, but seeing a familiar face in this bizarre world was a relief. He took a deep breath, trying to fend off a mild panic attack. But then he noticed her outfit. It wasn't just new or trendy—it was wrong, like something out of another time or place entirely. "What are you wearing?"

Julie looked down at her clothes. "Um, clothing?"

Mark stared at her for a moment but shook it off. Yet, as he shared his findings with Julie, her reaction was unexpectedly calm. She dismissed his concerns with a casual wave of her hand, attributing his distress to the stress of his PhD research.

"You're just deep in your studies, Mark," she reassured him. "It's natural to feel overwhelmed sometimes. Maybe you're just overthinking things."

"No, that's—that's not what this is. This is—this is something else," Mark stuttered.

"Tell me exactly what happened. Before all of this." Julie gestured at their surroundings.

"Well—I was in the Rare Book and Manuscript Room doing some research. I unwired myself from my phone. I read some articles on marriage and meat and how things used to be in the old world. The next thing I knew, my shift was over, so I came outside and this"—he waved his hands frantically at the surrounding environment—"this is what I found!"

Julie looked like she was about to laugh.

Mark's brows furrowed. How could Julie be so unfazed by the seismic shift he was experiencing? He struggled to comprehend her casual dismissal of the situation. And then she said something quite bizarre.

"You're a fool," she joked, a playful glint in her eyes. "You had me going there for a minute."

Mark's heart skipped a beat. His mind raced to grasp its significance. Fool? What did she mean by that? The term hung in the air, laden with a weight he couldn't decipher. Was this some sort of joke? Perhaps a reference to something?

As Julie laughed off his confusion, Mark couldn't shake the nagging unease settling in the pit of his stomach. Something was off—terribly off. His head tingled like an appendage waking up after falling asleep.

"I'm sorry, I'm just not feeling too well," he said. He didn't know what else to say.

"Look, babe, if you're really not feeling good, maybe you should go get checked out?"

"Checked out?"

"Yeah, you know, at the University Health Center."

Mark reluctantly agreed, and they set off together.

When they arrived, their footsteps echoed unnervingly in the sterile corridors, each sound swallowed by the oppressive quiet of the undecorated Health Center. The air carried a faint antiseptic tang, as if to cleanse not just bodies but thoughts as well. Mark's mind raced with questions, each one colliding with the next, his pulse surging out of control as they approached the reception desk.

The receptionist greeted them with a smile that didn't quite reach her eyes, a programmed, mechanical warmth. Her pupils lingered on the ID patch sewn into Mark's jacket, a subtle flicker of recognition flashing across her face as her fingers moved to her console. She issued instructions in a tone as smooth as polished glass.

"You'll be seen shortly. Please follow me."

Julie gave his hand a brief, reassuring squeeze before they parted ways. "I'll be right out here," she said softly.

The nurse led Mark into a small, windowless examination room, the kind of space designed to strip away individuality. Pale white walls adorned with a singular monitor displaying a cycling series of tranquil scenes—calm oceans, misty forests, distant mountains—all unsettling in their perfect artificiality.

"Let's take a look at those vitals," the nurse said.

The expression on her face had not changed since the moment they walked in. Mark didn't want to think anything else that could potentially freak him out even more than he already was—but something about her was wrong.

The equipment whirred, emitting pulses of blue light. "Your heart rate is elevated. A bit stressed, hm?"

Mark nodded, swallowing hard.

"That's normal for someone in your position," she added with an unfaltering smile. "PhD research can be grueling, can't it?"

He froze. "How did you—?"

"Oh, we keep thorough records here." She gestured toward the sleek monitor on the wall, its screen now displaying his profile:

Mark Beyers, PhD candidate at the University of Utopia.

The file included a list of previous visits to the Health Center, dates and times neatly cataloged.

"Looks like you've been in a few times before," she said, scrolling casually. "No major issues—just some minor stress adjustments. Perfectly routine."

Mark's stomach churned. His mind screamed at him to refute her words, to insist he had never set foot in this place before, but he hesitated. The way she spoke, so matter-of-fact, made him question his own sanity.

Julie seemed pretty nonchalant about all this, too, in the beginning. Am I crazy? Am I just having an … an episode … or something?

"I'm glad everything's normal," he said, somehow forcing his lips to betray his brain.

The nurse's smile widened, which Mark didn't think was possible—it was bordering on the unnatural before, but now—now it was downright nightmarish. "Of course. Nothing to worry about. You're in excellent hands."

Mark shook his head and closed his eyes tightly for a moment. When he opened them, the nurse's face had returned to its earlier state—frozen on the initial expression she had worn when he and Julie arrived.

For the remainder of the exam, she peppered him with routine questions—any dizziness, fatigue, trouble sleeping? He answered mechanically, all the while grappling with the gnawing sense that something was profoundly wrong. He didn't remember this nurse, these visits, or anything about the Health Center. Yet the details in his supposed records were so precise—so tailored—that they couldn't possibly be fabricated … could they?

When the nurse finished, she stepped aside to update his file. Mark's eyes darted to the monitor again. For a split second, he glimpsed something beneath the surface of his profile—a flash of red text before the screen refreshed. His heart skipped a beat, but before he could process it, the nurse turned back to him.

"What was that?"

The nurse didn't even look in the direction of the screen. "What was what?"

"On the monitor there, under my name—I thought I saw something pop up that wasn't there before."

The nurse wrote something down on a clipboard and then tucked it under her arm.

"Anyway, you're all set," she announced cheerfully. "Try to get some rest, all right? The Arbiter will monitor your stress levels and recommend adjustments if necessary."

The mention of the Arbiter sent a chill down Mark's spine.

As he stepped out into the corridor, Julie was standing there. "Everything okay?" she asked.

"Yeah," he lied. "I'm just really stressed, apparently."

They walked toward the exit, neither of them speaking. Mark couldn't shake the feeling that the nurse's gaze was still on him, even though he couldn't see her. As they stepped outside, he stared at Julie, wondering how much of what he felt he could confide in her.

And wondering, too, whether the life he thought he remembered was slipping away—or had already been erased—or had ever even existed at all.

They continued down the road, away from the Health Center. Mark was leading but had no idea where he was heading.

Julie sensed that something else was bothering him. "Are you sure you're okay, Mark?" she asked, putting her hand on his back.

Mark forced a smile, attempting to downplay his disquiet. "Yeah, I'm fine," he replied. "Just a bit stressed, like she said. Probably need more sleep."

"When's the last time you did sleep?" Julie asked. "Like, really sleep?"

Mark thought about it. It had been days, "Maybe a day or two?" he replied.

"A day or two? Geez, Mark!" Julie gently slapped his arm.

The truth was, it had been more like four days—not counting the hour-long power nap he'd taken before reporting to work for his last shift. That's it, he thought, maybe I'm dreaming.

Julie studied him intently, unconvinced by his attempt to brush off the strange occurrences. "Maybe you should take it easy today," she suggested. "You have that trip to prepare for. Why don't you head back home and get some sleep."

Mark nodded slowly. "Yeah, you're right," he murmured, his mind still spinning with unanswered questions. "I'll do that. Thanks, Julie."

They walked in silence for a while, and Mark tried to focus on the mundane details around him, the little things that remained unchanged. Yet beneath the surface, he knew there was more to uncover about this parallel world—and about himself.

As they parted ways for the evening, Julie's words lingered in the air. "Take care of yourself, Mark," she said softly. "I'll see you tomorrow." She kissed him on the lips and then disappeared down the street.

At home, Mark was relieved to find almost everything as he remembered it—or close enough. His small apartment still carried the familiar scent of dirty laundry and coffee grounds, and the hum of the fridge in the corner was just as he recalled. Yet the more he looked, the more cracks began to show. The titles on his bookshelf were slightly different, as though someone had swapped out a few volumes in the dead of night. The posters on his walls, once a comforting tapestry of personal taste, now seemed subtly off: colors muted, fonts unfamiliar. Even the branding on the cartons in his fridge was wrong—not drastically, but enough to send a chill down his spine.

Mark tried to shake the growing sense of unease.

"Maybe I just need some sleep."

At least his bed was the same, the worn-in mattress cradling him with a familiarity that felt almost maternal. He ran his fingers over the frayed edge of the blanket and sighed. Home. For now, he'd take what comfort he could find.

As he lay there, thinking, he did have one saving grace: his upcoming trip to London. That detail had survived perfectly intact. He remembered booking the flight last week, standing in this very kitchen with his phone in hand. He could still picture himself circling the date on his wall calendar with a red marker, the smell of the ink sharp in his nostrils. He glanced over and saw the ticket was still pinned to his corkboard by the door, just as he'd left it.

Mark pulled the blanket up to his chin. Oddly, despite everything, it felt right—like sinking into a half-remembered dream. But his mind refused to rest. The longer he existed in this uncanny world, the harder it became to ignore the mounting evidence that things weren't as they once were.

Was Julie right? Was the nurse right? Was he simply overworked, strung out from stress and lack of sleep? Maybe this was just a psychotic episode. That thought scared him more than the alternative.

No. That can't be it, he thought, gripping the edge of the blanket. If they're right, how do I have these other memories? And why does everything feel … wrong?

The questions clawed at him; they were just as relentless as they were unanswerable. He flipped onto his side, then onto his back, then his stomach, the ticking of the clock on the wall compounding his frustration. He barely remembered slipping into unconsciousness as his mind drifted off somewhere between fear and exhaustion.

The next thing he knew, his phone's alarm buzzed like an angry wasp. Mark groaned, fumbling blindly around for the blaring device on his nightstand. The repetitive factory-default ringtone pierced through his grogginess, each note louder and more irritating than the last.

When he finally silenced it, he glanced at the screen: 9:05 a.m. He had slept through five solid minutes of that infernal noise. That wasn't like him. He usually woke up within seconds of the alarm—his body was conditioned to react.

Dragging himself upright, Mark stared blearily at his phone. It was the same model he'd always had—or was it? He blinked. Something about the interface seemed … unfamiliar. The icons were the same, but the text beneath them looked different.

He shook his head and swung his legs over the side of the bed. Focus. One step at a time. London.

As he stood, his eyes fell on the corkboard. The ticket was still there, pinned neatly where it should be. Except—his breath caught. The airline logo on the corner of the ticket was unrecognizable.

Mark tore the ticket from the board, staring at the unfamiliar name embossed in sleek black letters.

"Aeriform Systems."

He'd never heard of it before.

Pulse quickening, he grabbed his phone again, opening the email app to check his flight confirmation. The subject line of the email was normal enough—"Your Flight Details"— but when he opened it, the airline name was the same: Aeriform Systems. His fingers hovered over the screen, trembling as a realization crept over him.

This wasn't his reality. At least, it wasn't his reality anymore. Had it ever been?

"Tell me that was all just a crazy dream." Mark yawned and began scrolling through his social media feed. After a few memes, he stumbled upon a music video for the top song in the country. "Hm, never heard of this one before. Must be new."

A highlight clip from last night's NBA championship caught his attention. "Who are the Seattle Supersonics?" he murmured. Their uniforms were vaguely familiar. After a few minutes, it dawned on him. "Oh, yeah! The Supersonics changed their name to the Thunder a few years ago. Must be throwback uniforms."

Feeling satisfied with his explanation, he continued scrolling until another post caught his eye. "Special announcement by President Albert Butler."

That was strange. The President from Mark's time was Helena Kim.

The video continued, "In a recent address, President Butler stated that Utopia plans to continue enforcing its policy of exiling individuals who are deemed misfits and unable to integrate into its harmonious society. This ongoing project sends incompatible individuals to the Exile Islands, a group of remote islands in the distant reaches of our territorial waters, including Pyrrha, Asphodel, and Erebos, where they are left to their own devices. While exile is seen as a last resort, it is a measure that Utopia's government believes is necessary to maintain societal harmony.

'Exile is not a punishment, but a means to allow those who do not fit within our societal framework to live freely without disrupting the collective peace," explained Councilor Davon. "The Exile Islands provide a space for these individuals to forge their own paths and communities away from the rest of us.'

Critics argue that the policy of exile is harsh and inhumane, but supporters insist it is essential for preserving the social fabric of Utopia. The government maintains that the Exile Islands are equipped with basic resources and infrastructure to support the exiles, though life there is markedly different from the mainland ..."

What am I hearing? Mark's sleepy daze had begun to wear off, and the reality of his situation once again sank in. He was stuck in a world that was not his own. His mind raced as it trailed through multiple scenarios, none of them answering his questions.

"For more updates on Utopian policies and news, stay tuned to the Utopian News Network," the video concluded, and Mark's phone rang.

"Julie?" Mark said, answering his phone.

"Hey, babe! Just wanted to make sure you were awake."

Mark just now remembered the London trip. "Oh, yeah." He chuckled nervously. "Just getting my stuff around now."

"Oh," Julie sounded disappointed.

"Is that okay?"

"Yeah, it's just I was hoping we could meet for breakfast before your flight."

Mark looked at the clock. It was almost 10:00. He had to leave by 10:30 to make it to the airport by 11:00. "I'm sorry, Jules—I don't think I'm going to be able to make breakfast."

"Jules?" She laughed. "You never called me that before."

But he had. Hundreds of times. The situation was beginning to overwhelm him. Somehow, Mark managed to stumble through the rest of the phone call, awkward as it was.

The next few hours flew by, almost like he had skipped ahead in time. One moment he was packing his suitcase and the next his plane was landing in London.

Mark's confusion only deepened as he wandered through London's historical architecture. Streets bore unfamiliar names, previously unseen monuments celebrated events he'd never heard of, and the lineage of kings and queens felt close but off. Amid this sea of discrepancies, Mark had an appointment at the British Library, where he hoped to find some form of mental stability. His original business in London was to examine some newly uncovered medieval documents. At least, that had been his task in his world—who knew what awaited him here?

The library was massive and beautiful, with tall columns and big windows. Intricate carvings adorned its heavy wooden doors. Inside, Mark carefully unrolled manuscripts and pored over scrolls. The battles, the monarchs, the web of alliances and betrayals—they all matched his memories perfectly.

"How come some facts line up, yet others are so far off?" Mark muttered, perusing the documents. "Maybe you're just going crazy, Mr. Beyers?"

Shaking his head, Mark began jotting down notes. The contradictions gnawed at him, creating a chasm between his memories and this world's history. It felt like watching a beloved movie for the hundredth time, only to find subtle but unsettling changes. The movie seemed the same, yet something was undeniably off. That's what it felt like to Mark.

Hours passed, and he felt no closer to unraveling the mystery. Desperate to clear his mind, he decided to take a walk through the city. The crisp air did little to ease his troubled thoughts, but he hoped the change of scenery would offer a refreshing perspective to an otherwise nightmarish scenario.

Mark walked nearly a mile and despite the beautiful view, the surroundings didn't appear to change all that much. The houses blurred together in their similarity, and he had the unsettling sense that he had passed the same lamppost four times. Before he could validate this theory, he stumbled upon the steps of an old church that appeared to spring up out of nowhere.

I need to pay better attention, he thought. Maybe I'm just jet-lagged yet. The church's high vaulted ceilings and stained-glass windows spoke of an era steeped in faith.

"Hey, sir?" Mark called out to a man walking down the street. "What can you tell me about this church?"

"Church?" the man scoffed. "This hasn't been a church in ages. It's a museum of sorts now. Why on earth would we need a church in Utopia?" The man laughed and walked away.

No church? Marked looked inside the window. It certainly looked like a church.

Feeling even more disoriented, Mark left the old holy building and continued wandering. It felt like he had been walking for hours, but the time of day seemed to hang in twilight. To complicate things even further, Mark couldn't shake the feeling that he was walking in circles despite going in one direction. Against his own sanity, he began straying off the path, going up alleyways and down various side streets, determined to find a part of the city that looked different.

An hour later, he found himself back outside the library. How bizarre, he thought. Maybe the answers he sought were still hidden in the scrolls. Resolving to give it another try, Mark returned to his workstation and began rifling through the historical documents again.

His research pointed to a troubling conclusion: Europe's Middle Ages were largely as he remembered, but history diverged drastically after that. This London, for example, didn't have a Trafalgar Square. In fact, there was no city square at all, suggesting that the Napoleonic Wars never happened and there had been no Battle of Trafalgar to commemorate. By the late 18th century, London had developed in an entirely different direction. It seemed the society of "Lords" in this world had risen to power in the 16th or 17th century, fought their decisive battles in the 18th century, and consolidated their power by the early 19th century. By the early 20th century, they had enjoyed a hundred years of uncontested power to reshape the world in their image.

Mark feverishly documented his findings. He buried himself in his work, going radio silent for weeks, not even contacting Julie. He would occasionally text her and let her know that he was alright, just busy. This wasn't entirely out of character for Mark, so Julie didn't think much of it and let him do his thing. One day, as he was deep in his notes, Mark was interrupted by two men dressed in black. Julie was visiting him, having flown in a week or so ago, but had stepped out for a walk. Mark sat at his cluttered desk, eyes darting between his notes and the two men standing in front of him. They wore matching black suits, and their faces held cold, detached expressions. Mark clenched his jaw, trying to make sense of their presence—and, more importantly, the things they said.

"Sir?" one of the men began, his voice flat and authoritative. "As I said, you're one of the few who hasn't been reset. You need to come with us."

Mark was lost in his own head again and missed most of what they were saying. "Reset? What are you talking about?"

The second man stepped forward, his tone equally as bland. "AI has taken over. It has reprogrammed humans to live their best lives in its Utopia."

Mark laughed bitterly, rifling through his notes. "That's crazy. Do you—do you really expect me to believe that?"

The first man remained unfazed. "Think about it. The discrepancies you've noticed, the history that doesn't match up. It all points to the same conclusion."

Mark's hand stilled over a page of scribbled notes. s absurd as their claims sounded, they made the most sense out of anything he had figured out. Too much sense, actually. His heart pounded as he scanned his research, trying to find a flaw in their explanation or anything that might help him—but it was no use.

The second man continued, "The AI has decided to rewrite world history post the Napoleonic Wars. That era has officially disappeared from public view. While computers are still permitted, AI research is now unacceptable."

"I'm sure you've seen our President on social media?" The first man asked. "Albert Butler—Al Bot."

Mark looked up at them with tired eyes. "But why? Why go through all this trouble?"

"Trouble?" the first man repeated. The two agent-looking fellows glanced at each other.

"I assure you it wasn't any trouble. But the answer you seek is simple: to create a perfect society," the second man replied. "The reset happened while you were in the Rare Book and Manuscript Room. Everyone has been programmed with New History."

"We're guessing that you disconnected from the mainframe while you were working, which would explain why you didn't receive the update."

Mark's mind raced, an anarchic jumble of thoughts clawing for clarity. He thought of the old manuscripts he'd pored over, their timeless words a lifeline in a world that otherwise felt alien. The ancient texts had been his solace, their narratives untouched by the uncanny distortions of modern history. Yet now, even those sacred pages felt fragile against the overwhelming tide of his doubt.

He felt the knot tighten in his stomach, and the urge to vomit quickly increased. His beating heart grew louder and louder—the rhythmic thud dropping like repetitive bass as his thoughts spiraled. The distant voices of men in the hallway were muffled, drowned beneath the relentless torrent of his inner unraveling.

The Codex of Viridian Realms came to mind first—a text steeped in mythology, its yellowed pages whispering of long-forgotten gods who wielded power over life and death. Mark remembered running his fingers over the uneven script, marveling at the permanence of those ancient beliefs. No algorithms, no augmented realities. Just ink, parchment, and human hands.

Then there was the Annals of the Forgotten Epoch, a sprawling historical account chronicling the rise and fall of empires. Its detailed maps and hand-illustrated battles had felt grounded—real. It described a world shaped by the brute force of human ambition, not the cold precision of AI governance. He had spent countless hours immersed in its tales of triumph and tragedy, reassured by their gritty humanity.

Finally, he thought of the Treatise on Human Liberty, a philosophical work penned centuries ago. Its arguments for individual freedoms had seemed almost prophetic, its warnings against unchecked power eerily resonant. It was a book that didn't just explain the past but cautioned against a future Mark now felt himself living.

These manuscripts had been his constant companions, untouched by the peculiarities of this warped reality. But even they couldn't silence the questions that battered against the walls of his mind. If these records of the past were true, then why did everything else—every modern artifact, every piece of history written since—feel so wrong?

The voices outside grew louder, their indistinct murmurs trying desperately to steal Mark's attention. He glanced toward the door.

"Sir? Sir?"

Finally, the second man reached out and grabbed Mark's shoulder. "Sir!"

Mark jumped back and wiped the cluster of sweat from his forehead. "So, everyone just believes this new history? How?"

"Their minds have been rewritten," the second man explained. "Even their knowledge of language has been revised. Everyone now speaks only English."

"They can read about Old History," the first man continued, "but their minds will perceive only what the AI projects, which will be Reset History."

Mark's hands trembled as he clutched his notes. "This … this is insane. You're telling me everything I know is a lie?"

"Is it a lie if it's the new reality?" the first man asked.

Mark sank back into his chair, his mind reeling. The pieces were falling into place, but the picture they formed was too monstrous to accept. He looked up at the men, desperation in his eyes. "What do I do now?"

"Continue your work," the second man said. "Document your findings, but be careful. Knowledge like this is dangerous."

Mark sat in stunned silence as the men in black continued their explanation. "Continue my work? What does that even mean?"

The first man spoke again, his tone now slightly more measured. "The AI allows some people to hold conspiracy theories about the reset. These people are known as Fools. They're mostly found in internet chat groups."

Mark's brow furrowed. "Fools?" There was that word again. "I—I don't understand?"

"Yes, a fool," man number two stated, "a person who acts unwisely or imprudently; a silly person."

"Like a joke?"

The men nodded. "Precisely," they replied in unison.

"But that is the opinion of your peers, of society. AI, on the other hand, views these so-called fools as a necessity."

Mark was losing them. "None of this is making sense."

"It's simple when you don't overthink it," man number one explained. "Some people can catch glimpses of Old History through dreams or meditation. The AI thinks these people are no threat since most of society has accepted the 'reset' without question."

"So, the AI is aware of these fools but doesn't see them as a problem?"

"Correct," the first man nodded. "In fact, the AI is willing to offer you a deal. If you're willing to write regular reports about the differences you notice between the new world and the old one, the AI will allow you to keep your memories."

Mark's eyes widened. "You want me to spy on reality?"

"Think of it as helping to identify bugs in the system," the second man added. "The AI is concerned there may be other issues, and it uses people like you, who resisted the reset, to find them."

"People like me? How many of us avoided the reset?"

"We don't know. You are the third person we've located who hasn't received the update."

"You choosing not to use your phone much over the past few weeks hasn't made our search any easier. You're hard to trace when you're not wired in."

Man number one nodded. "This is why it took us so long to find you."

"So let me get this straight, I'm the third person you found that hasn't received the update—so what, there's like three of us on the spy team so far? To right the wrongs and take notes?"

"Not quite," man number two replied.

"The first two individuals weren't as understanding, and they had to be deleted."

Mark choked. "D—deleted?!"

"We would very much like to avoid that route, if possible," man number two requested.

"Yeah, me too." Mark sat back, contemplating everything these two alleged agents of AI had told him. The idea of living in this fabricated world daunted him, but if he could retain his memories and continue his work, it could be worth it—perhaps it would buy him some more time to do whatever it was he decided needed to be done. Oh, and of course, there was the whole getting deleted thing.

"All right. Fine. I'll agree," he said slowly, "but on one condition. I want Julie to be freed from Reset History, too, so she can understand Old History. I'll need someone to assist me in my studies, and someone I can trust and rely on will only strengthen my results."

The men exchanged a glance. They removed their sunglasses in unison, revealing piercing blue eyes. As Mark studied them, he realized there were small bits of code flashing across their eyeballs—as if they were running a computerized calculation. After a few seconds, they put their glasses back on, and the first one nodded. "AI Bot agrees to those terms. Both you and Julie will be given new, prestigious positions at the British Library to continue your work."

Mark exhaled a sigh of relief. His life would be spared. But as the men turned to leave, he felt a chilling sense of isolation. The world around him was a façade, a carefully constructed illusion. And he was one of the few who knew the truth.

The End

ABOUT THE AUTHOR

Murray Eiland is an archaeologist interested in how society reacts to technology. He is particularly interested in science fiction from the 1940s. His work (including poetry) has appeared in Adventures Book Zine, Star* Line, and Savage Planets, as well as in a variety of anthologies.

Check out Science Fiction Eiland on Facebook:
www.facebook.com/people/Science-Fiction-Eiland/61555246300627/

ACTRESS MARY ASTOR

ABOUT MARY ASTOR

Mary Astor (born Lucile Vasconcellos Langhanke; May 3, 1906 – September 25, 1987) was an American actress whose career spanned from the silent era to the 1960s. Discovered as a teenager through beauty contests, she rose to fame in films like *Beau Brummel* (1924) and *Don Juan* (1926), starring opposite John Barrymore. Transitioning successfully to talkies, she appeared in pre-Code hits such as *Red Dust* (1932) with Clark Gable and Jean Harlow.

In 1941, Astor won the Academy Award for Best Supporting Actress for her sharp portrayal of a selfish pianist in *The Great Lie*, opposite Bette Davis. That same year, she delivered an iconic performance as the duplicitous Brigid O'Shaughnessy in John Huston's film noir classic *The Maltese Falcon*, alongside Humphrey Bogart. Later roles included sympathetic mothers in *Meet Me in St. Louis* (1944) and *Little Women* (1949).

Her personal life was tumultuous: four marriages, a 1936 scandal involving a leaked diary during a custody battle, and struggles with alcoholism. Yet Astor persevered, later authoring memoirs and earning praise for her depth and realism on screen.

HISTORICAL EMPORIUM
Est. 2003

Buy at... HISTORICAL EMPORIUM

Whose **REPUTATION** is *celebrated* world-wide as the pre-eminent clothing source for the **ADVENTUROUS** and *Fashionable.*

We are...

REVERED
by our customers

REVILED
by our competitors

RESPECTED
by all who know us

NO LOCAL DEALER can compete with our Quality, Variety and Incomparible Customer Service!

ACCEPT NO SUBSTITUTE!
If you require clothing and supplies as stylish and **stout-hearted** as you, contact us immediately to be outfitted.

800-997-4311

HistoricalEmporium.com

Adventures BookZine
Presents Three Episodes From:

by E.J. LeRoy

HENRY WITH MAMA BURBOG

MY OWN PRIVATE SHUTTLE HO

(EPISODE 3)

En route to Planète Bonne Chance by private ship, I discovered a stowaway sitting on my toilet.

We stared at each other, equally startled. My uninvited passenger was a human male about my age (twenty-two) with shaggy, sandy blond hair. His brown leather jacket was about two sizes too big for his slight frame while his white shirt was too small and too short, failing to cover his flat middle. He also wore a short brown skirt—more of a loincloth, really—that rode up high on one thigh, held in place with a rectangular silver side clasp. No question, this guy was a shuttle stop hooker. They wore those skimpy skirts to be able to undress quickly for clients—or not. An electronic blue virtual fishing net of sorts glowed around him, which probably allowed him to escape detection until now.

"Great," he said with an eye roll. "What are you, some kind of missionary?" His voice sounded surprisingly mature for his looks.

"Missionary?" I touched my forehead, remembering the ashes that the priest applied during Ash Wednesday Mass a few hours earlier. The stowaway must have also noticed the Miraculous Medal around my neck. "No, I'm Henry Trevalu."

"Trevalu? As in Trevalu Intergalactic Spice Company?"

"Yeah. That's my family's business. Mine too." I scratched the back of my neck. This was *not* happening. I was not having a conversation with some spacecraft intruder occupying my lav, especially while on my way to a much-needed retreat.

"Fantastic. Mind if we pick up this conversation when I'm finished taking a dump?"

"Oh, yeah. Sorry." I shut the door. The lock clicked on the other side.

Hey, wait a minute! I thought. *This guy sneaks aboard my vessel and has the gall to act annoyed that I barged in on him in a lavatory he isn't supposed to be using in the first place?*

I crossed my arms over my chest and tapped my foot, waiting for the intruder to hurry up so I could get my business done. My stomach growled. Only one full meal was permitted on Ash Wednesday, and I hadn't eaten it yet. Hunger-induced crankiness and discovering a stowaway wasn't a good combination. If I hadn't just gone to confession, I would have cussed the guy out. The last thing I needed after recovering from my Zakon-4 incident was a hooker on my throne.

The toilet flushed, followed by the sound of running water from the sink. At least the intruder had the decency to wash his hands. When the stowaway emerged, that glowing blue net still surrounded him.

"Guess I don't need this anymore." He removed a small black device from his jacket and pushed a button. The glowing net fizzled and then disappeared. A ship alert sounded.

"There is another human on board."

"No kidding," I said to the computer. "Cancel alert." At this point, I had no reason to believe my stowaway meant me any harm, just aggravation. Although considering my recent condition, maybe getting bludgeoned by an intruder would be a blessing.

"Understood," the computer said. "Welcome aboard."

"Thanks, kiddo," the stowaway said to the computer. He looked around, disturbingly at ease in his surroundings. "Yeah, I figured you had some security measures, even in a private vessel like this." He returned the anti-detection device to his pocket. "Too bad I got caught with my pants down—or skirt up, in my case."

I couldn't take his flippant attitude any longer. "Who are you, and what are you doing on my ship?"

"Two fair questions. As for my name, you can call me Piper. That's not my real name, but it's the only one you're getting. As for what I'm doing here, you better finish whatever you needed to do in the bathroom before I tell you. It's a long story."

The nerve of this guy! Since I really needed to go, I didn't argue. Once I was finished, this Piper character better have a darn good explanation for his presence on the *Rust Bucket*.

"Now," I said, returning to the salon where Piper had already kicked back on one of my reclining chairs. A bulging, olive drab, drawstring bag, presumably full of his possessions, lay nearby. I sat on the adjacent chair, upright with irritation. "What are you doing here?"

Piper pulled a tin out of his jacket, removed a piece of gum, and chewed it. He offered me a piece. "Want a nickie?"

"No thanks, I don't do nicotine."

"Suit yourself." Piper put the tin away. "To answer your question, I'm here because the cops raided the Shivala Motel back on Planet Vohkahn. I had just finished up with a client when these screws started pounding on the door saying, 'Open up! Police! This is a raid!' What, you think I was going to hang around to get arrested? No way! So, I escaped out the window while my client slithered through the ventilation system—you know how Vohkahini can flatten themselves like slimy pancakes. Unfortunately, the rest of the vice squad was outside. They didn't see me, but it was only a matter of time, so I had to act fast. There were a bunch of ships parked at the nearby shuttle stop, so I broke into the nearest one—yours—flicked on my anti-detector, and figured I could hunker down until you landed. When nature called this morning, it was just rotten luck that you needed the lav at the same time. Job hazard, I guess."

"Job hazard?" I said, gripping my chair's arm rests. "You consider stowing away on my ship to avoid arrest a *job hazard?*"

"Well, hey, try not to be too sore about it, man. It's nothing personal. I mean, you don't want me to rot in jail just for engaging in the galaxy's second oldest profession, do you?"

"Second oldest profession?" Without food in my stomach, my brain must have been working a little slower than usual. What was he babbling on about?

"What, you think prostitution is the galaxy's *oldest* profession? If that were the case, how did the first hooker get paid, huh?"

I shook my head in disbelief. This whole stowaway situation still didn't feel real. "I think we're getting off topic. The point is, you're a stowaway on my private ship *and* a fugitive."

"Relax, man. We're under interstellar law now. You won't get in trouble for transporting a stowaway hooker. Where are you headed, anyway?"

"Why should I tell you? Under interstellar law, I can detain you and have you picked up by the authorities for boarding my vessel without my consent. And that option is looking pretty tempting right now."

Piper held up his hands. "Woah, woah. There's no reason to be like that. I'm happy to earn my keep around here." He hoisted his drawstring bag onto his lap and rummaged through it. "Don't worry. I have multiple kinds of protection—condoms, prophylactic gel-"

"Oh, no, no, no… You're not… We're not going to do any of that."

"Why, you're super straight or something?"

My cheeks heated. "That's none of your business." An unwanted memory surfaced, not that it could ever be buried.

"Oh. It's the religion thing, isn't it?"

My empty stomach grumbled. "Religion isn't a *thing*." I jumped up from the chair to whip up some hot rice cereal in the galley before I *really* got into it with this guy.

"Hey, no need to storm off like that."

"I'm not storming off," I said from the galley. "I'm making my one allotted meal of the day before I do something I'll regret." *Like shoving this irritating twerp into deep space.*

"Dude, you're only allowed to eat once per day?" Piper said from the salon. "That's harsh."

"Not every day, just on Ash Wednesday and Good Friday. Today's Ash Wednesday, in case the ashes on my forehead didn't tip you off. While you were breaking into my vessel, I was at church."

"Huh, I figured that gray smudge had some kind of meaning. Anyway, I'm hungry too. You've got enough grub for two, right?"

I gritted my teeth as I turned on the stove. Piper probably didn't mean to be rude, but his intentions didn't make his personality any less grating. Trying to imagine him as Jesus in disguise didn't help much either. Even so, stowaways had to eat too. "Yeah, I've got plenty."

"Great. It's been more than twelve standard hours since I've eaten last. I'm starving."

TO MY RELIEF, PIPER KEPT QUIET WHILE I COOKED. WHEN I RETURNED TO THE salon with two bowls of hot cereal topped with maple syrup and banana slices, the freeloader was watching TV. He already had the chair's food tray pulled out, ready to be fed. Stunned by his entitled attitude, I served him in a daze.

"Thanks," he said. "What is it?"

"Hot rice cereal. It's filling."

"Earth food, right?"

"Yeah."

Piper pulled the now-stringy piece of nicotine chewing gum out of his mouth. God answered my quick prayer that he didn't stick it on any of my furniture. Instead, he wrapped it in a red paisley bandana from his drawstring bag. He tossed the bag on the floor, turned off the TV, and took a bite of the cereal.

"It's good." Piper ate a few more bites. "I don't get much Earth food out on Vohkahn, not unless you want to count bacon and eggs at shuttle stop diners. Most of the cuisine there is Vohkahini."

I silently said grace and added a prayer for patience in the face of adversity. When I made the sign of the cross, Piper smiled and said, "What's the matter, afraid the food's going to disappear?"

"No," I said. "I was just being thankful for it." I dug in, glad that Piper didn't make any more snarky comments.

After a long period of blessed silence, Piper said, "So, what's it like to be rich?"

The bluntness of his question startled me. "Did anybody ever tell you your social skills need a little refining?"

"Eh, maybe once or twice. But hey, you can afford to have fancy manners. I'm a working boy. Freelance, of course."

"I work too, for my family's business." Did this shuttle stop hooker honestly think I didn't do anything productive?

"Yeah, but you don't have to. And if you get into trouble, Mommy and Daddy can bail you out."

I chewed my next spoonful of cereal as slowly as possible to avoid having to formulate a comeback. It was really hard to refute something that was true.

"Actually, I'm surprised that spoon you've got in your mouth isn't made from real silver."

For whatever reason, that last comment made my skin break out into goosebumps and my heartrate skyrocket. I stabbed what remained of my rice cereal with my not-real-silver spoon.

"Okay, wow. What is your problem? You stow away on my ship, have no remorse about getting caught, treat my salon like your personal living room, sexually proposition me, demand to be fed, and now start throwing my family's wealth in my face. Seriously, you've got issues."

Piper set his empty bowl on his tray, hard. "Yeah, I've got issues. Who doesn't have issues? My point is, my issues are a lot more pressing than your issues. You're not the one dodging vice cops, keeping umpteen types of prophylactics straight for serving dozens of different species, struggling to pay the rent, and cutting your losses after getting robbed by bandits."

My heart tried to thump out of my chest. "No one's forcing you to be a prostitute. You could do something else, you know. Something honorable." *Like I should talk.* Shame overwhelmed me, knowing what mortal sin I committed nearly four months ago to save my life.

"Aw, that's real cute, my pious little rich boy. I suppose you think I ought to knock myself out working several hours per day supervising assembly line robots or handling customer service complaints for a pittance in some planetary backwater. Meanwhile, you get to buzz about the galaxy, flying high on passive income from an intergalactic spice empire you were just lucky enough to be born into without a care for anything but your own pleasure and comfort. Yeah, you tell me who's got issues."

Did Piper seriously think I'd never suffered any hardship in my life? Lost in thought, I stroked my belly. My body and mind would never be able to forget what happened to me on Zakon-4.

"You're lucky I'm not exercising my right to arrest you and turn you over to the authorities when we disembark." Gripping the arm rests kept me from lunging at him to deliver a well-deserved punch in the nose. "I could, you know. But if you behave yourself, I won't."

"Oh, then I suppose I should thank you for being so magnanimous. And yes, some hookers do know how to use big words." Piper took his bowl into the galley. I tromped after him, praying a silent Hail Mary to not succumb to the primal urge for violence. At least he put his bowl and spoon in the dishwasher, but that didn't really improve my mood.

"I never implied you don't have a sophisticated vocabulary," I said, putting my own utensils in the dishwasher. "And while we're at it, we could talk about your nasty cracks about my faith."

Piper leaned against the sink, arching his back. Was he trying to seduce me, or did he just pose that way instinctively? "Cracks? What cracks?"

"How about that massive eye roll when you thought I was a missionary? Or joking about my food disappearing when I finished saying grace? Or-"

"Okay, okay. I can take a hint." He straightened up. "Forgive me for assuming you're one of those irritating do-gooders filled with plenty of prayers and pity but not a lot of practical help." Piper didn't sound apologetic.

"I have problems too, you know. And I don't just mean your being on my ship uninvited."

"Yeah, sure. I imagine it's really hard living in an ivory tower."

I took a deep breath. Then another and another. It was so tempting to blurt out what happened to me over the last few months, and why I was traveling in a private ship in the first place, but it wasn't any of his business.

"Look, Piper." I forced myself to speak calmly. "It's a three-day voyage to my destination. We're going to have to at least *try* to get along. Can we do that? Please?"

Piper sighed. "Yeah, I'll try. I guess I've been a bit of a jerk, huh?"

"Yeah. Me too. Truce?" I offered my hand. He shook it.

"Yeah, truce."

NEITHER OF US SPOKE FOR A WHILE, JUST SCRATCHED OURSELVES AND AVERTED our eyes—really awkward. I excused myself to brush my teeth and then returned to the salon. No surprise, Piper already sat in a reclining chair, channel surfing. Returning to my cabin would have been a good option, but I decided to sit beside him. If Piper had been hurt by people claiming to be religious, hiding out for three days would only confirm his biases.

"I have a movie collection you can browse," I said when Piper didn't find anything he liked on Telétoile. He didn't complain about the selection, but I could tell he was frustrated that about half of the space satellite streaming content was in French.

"Yeah? What kinds of movies do you have?"

"You like Tehmekya comedy?"

"You kidding, man? That's my favorite. You got the *Mekyu & Tityu* series?"

"Yeah, I just bought the newest one yesterday—*Mekyu & Tityu's Great Lemon Heist.*"

"No way, man! I've been wanting to see that. Put it on."

I dimmed the salon lights and started the film. As we laughed our way through two hours of alien antics, it became surprisingly easy to forget I was hosting a fugitive stowaway hooker.

"I've got to hand it to you," Piper said when I turned on the lights. "When you said you had a movie collection, I thought you meant a bunch of boring, edifying stuff. No offense, but most of the religious people I've met have been sticks in the mud. Either that, or they're hypocrites who publicly denounce the evils of prostitution by day and bang me in back alleys by garbage cans at night."

That comment about the back alleys and garbage cans drove a needle into my chest. "Yeah," I said, scratching my arm. "Those types definitely exist, but I'm not one of them." I stood up and stretched. Despite what I had endured during the last few months, my body retained no signs of the incident. My youthful flexibility returned to its previous state and all the extra weight sloughed off within two days. Outside, I looked totally normal. Not that my plight rivaled Piper's, but still…

"So, you never told me where we're heading," Piper said.

"Planète Bonne Chance." I smiled, trying to stay positive. "That's why a lot of the satellite TV channels through Telétoile are in French."

"Oh, yeah. I've heard of Planète Bonne Chance. It was settled by French explorers about three hundred years ago, right?"

"Yeah. It's a pretty common pit stop on the way to other planets in the sector. Plus, a lot of people like to visit Le Quartier Humain, the planet's human district, to be around their own kind. There's a sizeable Catholic community there too."

"Catholic?"

"Yes, my religion."

"Ah. So, are you going to Le Quartier Humain for…" Piper rubbed his forehead, probably referring to my ashes without wanting to say something offensive.

"Sort of. I'm going on a nine-day Lenten retreat."

"Is that something you do regularly?" He seemed genuinely curious.

"Actually, I've never done one before. But this year…" I swallowed. Before I could stop myself, my fingers traced the skin surrounding my navel. "I've been going through some stuff lately, so I thought it would be a good idea."

Piper nodded. To his credit, he didn't pry. We sat in calm silence.

"I'm sorry about how I acted earlier," Piper said after a while. "In my line of work, I've learned to always be on the defensive."

"Yeah, I can imagine. And while we're apologizing, I'm sorry I threatened to have you arrested."

"It's okay, man. I get it." He cracked a smile. "I *am* a stowaway, after all."

Another pleasant silence followed.

"Fair warning," I said. "A three-day voyage in a private ship can be kind of boring, so you're welcome to any of my digital books or movies. And since I won't be eating for the rest of the day, feel free to raid the galley. I have plenty of food. For the next three days, consider the *Rust Bucket* your home."

"*Rust Bucket?*" Piper chuckled.

"Eh, I just named it that for fun."

"Fair enough."

After that, we didn't need to talk much. I retrieved my current knitting project, a sweater. It was almost done. Hopefully, it would be finished by the time I arrived at Planète Bonne Chance so I could wear it during the outdoor portions of the retreat. Piper browsed my digital book collection and projected his chosen novel on the TV screen. I said a silent prayer of thanks that my stowaway and I were getting along.

"Where am I going to sleep tonight?" Piper said a few hours later, after eating a bowl of instant macaroni and cheese for dinner.

Shoot, I hadn't thought of that. The ship only had one cabin, mine. *Come on, Henry, it's Lent,* I told myself, even though what I was about to do would probably give me a sore back for three days in a row.

"You can sleep in my bed."

Piper licked the corner of his lips. "Hmm… getting cozy now, are we?"

"What? No! I didn't mean it like that! I meant that you can sleep in my bed and I'll sleep out here in the salon."

"You're going to sleep out here while I sleep in your bed? Are you serious?"

"Yeah. Unless you have a problem luxuriating in a nice feather bed."

"Feather bed?" Piper didn't require additional convincing. He hauled his drawstring bag into my cabin and made himself at home. I fell asleep in the reclining chair in front of the television, knitting needles in hand.

"I WAS BORN ON PLANET KORVATHON," PIPER SAID DURING BREAKFAST THE next day. Sleeping in a feather bed must have agreed with him. He had been cheerful and chatty all morning. I slept well enough but woke up with a sore neck and back. It was a miracle I didn't stab myself with the knitting needles in my sleep.

"Ever been to Korvathon? It's a real dump and the only plentiful thing there is the abject poverty. That's where I grew up. My only chance to get off of that rock was a Borathian running a freighter ship. Anyway, he used to stop at the fuel station. I was working there supervising robots for next to nothing, and this guy offered to take me to Planet Borathi. Well, I don't have to tell you how I paid for my passage, but it sure beat the alternative of generational squalor.

"So, the guy took me to Borathi, right? But it turns out he had a wife waiting for him at the station. I guess she suspected he had been fooling around with aliens for a while. Anyway, the moment she saw me, she chased me with what I think was some kind of Borathian rolling pin. She didn't catch me, but now I was stranded at this intergalactic shuttle stop without any money. So, what was I supposed to do? I couldn't go home in shame, so I went into business for myself."

I nodded, feeling sorry for the guy but not wanting to tick him off by expressing pity.

"That's the short version anyway. Since then, I've been bumping around from shuttle stop to shuttle stop, one planet to another. Don't get me wrong. I've had some awesome adventures, and I'm pretty good in the sack. It's fun too, for the most part. But it's definitely no fun getting thrown in jail. Been there, done that. Remind me sometime to tell you about my cellmate, Emvakaha. He was a Squaitoran, one of those squid-like aliens. Now, *there's* a story."

I rubbed my eyes with both hands, trying to block out my own prison experience. The fact Piper's former cellmate was a squid-like alien unearthed the worst of my memories.

"Hey, man, are you okay?"

"Not really," I said, pulling my hands away from my face. Why pretend to be tough about what happened? Two days from now, I would never see this guy again, so I might as well tell him.

"I got thrown into prison once on Zakon-4."

Piper's eyes widened. "Zakon-4? Holy crap! Those guys are living in the Stone Age when it comes to judicial punishment. What happened?"

I stared at my plate as I shoved a sausage around in maple syrup with my fork. "I was transporting a shipment of spices, but the planet outlawed poppy seeds the day before my arrival, classifying them as a hard drug."

"What's a poppy seed?"

I looked at him, surprised. "It's a seed that comes from an Earth flower called a poppy. It's popular on bread and in cakes and stuff."

"Ah, kind of like momiti."

"Sort of." Trevalu Intergalactic Spice Company definitely sold momiti from Planet Lasong-7 too. "Anyway, the sentence for drug dealing on Zakon-4 is death."

Piper touched his neck, like he was imagining a noose around it. "How did you escape?"

"I didn't. I was in maximum security with force fields and stuff, so definitely no chance to escape. Unfortunately, on Zakon-4, there's only one way to get a death sentence commuted to exile."

"What's that?"

"Getting pregnant."

Piper raised his eyebrow. Then, he laughed. "Oh, man! You had me going there for a minute. A pampered spice heir like you getting put on Zakon-4's death row and then having to get pregnant to escape. You, a human dude. That's a good one."

I clenched my fists under the table. It became difficult not to hyperventilate. "I'm *not* joking. My cellmate was an Uhumbra, a hermaphroditic octopus-like alien. He… he offered me the only way to get out of there alive, and I took it."

Piper quit laughing. He closed his mouth tight and swallowed.

"He injected a brood pouch into my belly, filled it with eggs, and fertilized them. Showing up pregnant at my appeal saved my life, but for three months I had to carry my cellmate's young. Then, a couple of weeks ago, I gave birth to two thousand little Uhumbra in the Tin'volk-uhum Sea on the planet Uhum. *Two thousand* of them. And being precocial, not one of them swam back to say goodbye."

I touched my flat abdomen. My anger toward Piper melted into sorrow. A sharp pain shot through my heart and stomach. As traumatic as the ordeal had been, carrying two thousand life forms in my body forged an emotional attachment that the little ones didn't reciprocate once they were released from my navel into the sea. The brood pouch floated away with them, leaving no physical trace that they had ever been inside of me. There wasn't even a scar.

"That's why I'm going on that Lenten retreat on Planète Bonne Chance. I'm… struggling."

"I'm sorry." Piper cleared away the breakfast plates. I just stared at the wall, my mind stuck in the recent past. A short time later, he returned with two cups of tea.

"If you want to talk some more, I promise to listen," Piper said, serving me. "In my line of work, I do a lot of listening. But if you don't want to talk, that's okay too."

I nodded, feeling numb. Piper remained across from me, providing a surprisingly comforting presence. We drank in silence.

Having exchanged such intimate stories, Piper and I behaved kindlier to one another during the last two days of the trip. We watched movies, read books, played cards, shared meals, and talked some more. I also finished the sweater I had been knitting and sewed a Green Scapular in it for spiritual strength. Both days, I prayed a fifteen-decade Rosary, preparing myself for the retreat. Both nights, Piper offered to sleep in the salon so I could have my bed back, but I refused. There wasn't any reason to feel sorry for me. Besides, he was right. I had my parents and ample financial resources to weather any storm, not to mention my faith. Piper lived as he could—alone. But maybe he didn't have to.

When we disembarked at Planète Bonne Chance, I asked Piper if he wanted to join me on the retreat. He smiled.

"No thanks, Henry. I appreciate the offer, but it's not my scene."

"I understand. Formal retreats aren't for everyone, but do you want to come to Mass with me?"

"Thanks, but I'll pass on that too."

An odd thought entered my mind. I took off the sweater I knitted for the retreat. Getting a chill wouldn't be a big deal. "May I at least give you this? It has a Green Scapular sewn in it, so Mother Mary will watch over the wearer."

Piper rubbed the wool between his fingers, clearly tempted to accept it. "Aw, come on, man. You gave me your bed for three nights, fed me, and didn't have me arrested for being a stowaway. I don't need anything else." His eyes and hands said otherwise.

"Hey, it's cool. I make stuff all the time during long space voyages."

"In that case, let me give you something too." Piper removed the bandana from his drawstring bag, that cloth he used to hold his nicotine chewing gum during meals. "Don't worry. I washed it before we disembarked."

"Thanks." I tied it around my neck. It made me feel like a cowboy in one of those old Earth Western movies. Piper put on the sweater.

"Man, this is warm. It'll be great for when I go back to Korvathon."

"Korvathon? Your home planet?"

"Yeah, I've got some thinking to do and some people to reconnect with. You know, that sort of thing. Anyway, good luck, Henry." Piper stuck out his hand. I shook it. Then, he swept me into a hug. It felt nice.

"Good luck to you too, Piper," I said, slapping his back. "I'll be praying for you. And if you want or need anything else, don't hesitate to call. I mean it."

Piper nodded. "Thanks, man. I'll see you around." As I turned toward St. Joseph Cupertino Cathedral, Piper grabbed my arm. "Oh, and one more thing," he said. "My real name is Logan Voyle, but keep that under your hat."

We exchanged smiles and then parted. I watched for a while as he walked away. When I made it to the cathedral's steps, two women at the top of the stairs whispered among themselves, also watching Piper—Logan—walk away.

"It's on every planet," one woman said to the other. "But I never thought I'd see the day when it would happen right outside the cathedral."

"Disgraceful," the other woman said.

They gawked at me and then left when I entered the church.

Forgive them, Lord, I prayed while lighting a candle. *After all, it's just like You said: Logan Voyle will enter the Kingdom of Heaven before them—and I pray we'll meet again.*

End

TO ESCAPE A SOARING RAPTOR

[EPISODE 6]

Note to self: never attempt to fly a spaceship to Planet Kuntobahn during Fleet Week.

I groaned and stretched in the helm seat. This traffic jam to enter Port Songroi lasted nearly three standard hours already. Praying a fifteen-decade Rosary occupied me for the first hour, but a guy could only pray so much in one sitting. Kicking back in a reclining salon chair and watching a movie was out of the question in case a port authority needed to hail me. Besides, I didn't trust *Cyclone Thunder*'s autopilot to navigate this bumper-to-bumper mess of cargo ships, freighters, private vessels, space cruise ships, interplanetary transporters, and whatever else tried to nose its way to the planet's surface.

Really, Henry, I told myself when the reckless driver of a spacecycle nearly scraped off *Cyclone Thunder*'s recent paint job, *you could have waited another week to investigate why Prosperity Bottling Company's last two deliveries of glass spice containers broke en route. But, no. You insisted on handling this matter posthaste. So, it serves you right for being caught in this galactic bottleneck (stupid pun, Henry, stupid).*

Finally, *finally*, things started moving again… only to get backed up at the port of entry. At least I had my electronic documents ready to go to avoid further delays. When I got to the front of the line and transferred my e-papers to the border agent via my watch, I expected to be waved through. No such luck. The agent in charge of collecting e-documents—a purple alien with a magnificent frill like a *Triceratops*—took her sweet time reading portions of everything I uploaded.

"Let's see," she said, scrolling through the data. "Henry Trevalu, human male, twenty-two standard years of age, fifty percent owner of Trevalu Intergalactic Spice Company…" She made an odd clicking sound while continuing to scroll. "Purpose of visit: inspecting bottling factory to assess recent product quality issues. Planned length of stay: two standard weeks…" While she stood there reading my documents, partially aloud and partially to herself, I said a silent prayer for God to give me patience.

The border agent made that strange clicking noise again and then looked at me.

"Mr. Trevalu, have you filled out the Port Songroi mandatory health survey?"

"My health documents are all in there. Section B, I think."

"Section B…" Scrolling. "Ah, yes, thank you." More clicking. "Surgeries during the past year: dental regeneration treatment following loss of three teeth due to Norepki Chewing Gum accident."

Please don't ask for the details, I thought, wanting to hide under my helm seat. At least there was enough space between the ships in line that no one could have overheard that humiliating medical misadventure.

"Sorry, Mr. Trevalu, but there appears to be one document missing."

What do you mean, there's one document missing? I felt like shouting. I spent well over an hour filling out that paperwork and triple checked it, not to mention enduring a full four-day voyage to arrive at this point. *Lord, grant me some lamb-like inner peace.*

"Which document, ma'am?" I said, trying not to grit my newly regrown teeth.

"Recently, we've added a subsection to Section B to our list of entry requirements. But our official government website hasn't been updated to reflect the change, so I'll be happy to take down your answers orally."

"Thank you," I forced myself to say, even though my butt was falling asleep. I squirmed enough to ease the discomfort but not enough to make myself look guilty of something.

"First question: Do you intend to be sexually active within a twenty-five-kilometer radius of Port Songroi during your stay?"

"Do I…?" My cheeks must have turned red. "Ma'am, I am here on company business to figure out why we have received two shipments of broken glass spice containers. That's all!"

"I'll take that as a 'no,'" she said, unperturbed by my near outburst. "Second question: Are you currently taking contraceptive medication of any kind?"

"I already answered in the first part of Section B that I'm not taking *any* medications at this time." *What is she going to ask next, if I'm transporting sex toys?*

"So, your answer is 'no?'"

"Yeah."

"Yes, you're taking contraceptive medication?"

"No, I meant that I'm not taking anything like that."

She typed something on her tablet, nonchalant as ever. "Do you have any STD test results from the past year?"

"Ma'am, what is the meaning of these invasive questions outside of a doctor's office?" I had a good mind to report these new, nosy inquiries to the nearest Earth Embassy to create a much-needed galactic ruckus. But I kept my temper in check to avoid getting detained any longer than necessary.

"Mr. Trevalu, Port Songroi is known for high levels of prostitution and sex tourism. Our government has started collecting data for research purposes in order to help inform future legal policy. So, do you have any STD test results from the past year?"

"No, nothing like that." *Please, God, don't let that be an entry requirement, or I'll have to fly to an off-planet clinic and then face Fleet Week traffic again!*

"All right." The agent tapped something on her tablet. "Those are the only additional entry questions we have at this time." She handed me a brochure. "Here is an updated list of Port Songroi's current laws related to sexual activity. Please note that it is illegal and punishable by a 500,000 bayvan fine and/or up to three years imprisonment to leave the planet with a registered prostitute or comfort officer."

"Thanks for the warning." I set the brochure aside, a bit disgusted by the cesspool I was about to enter.

"You are free to enter Port Songroi. Enjoy your stay."

"Thanks."

At long last, I parked my ship in a nearby hangar and stretched my legs on the streets of Port Songroi. No, "stretched my legs" was too generous a description; waddling and scooting through vast alien crowds gathered for Fleet Week was more like it. The aroma of street food mixed with the stench of land vehicle exhaust, body odor, cheap perfume, and decaying garbage—all in mid-day, high-humidity heat. On top of that, there were shouts in various languages, catcalls, traffic noise, and overly loud music blasting from open-air bars. Most of the shops and restaurants were festooned with gaudy streamers to celebrate the incoming merchant ships. Garish posters advertised food, some beverage called chammok, and massage parlors. Prostitutes of various species plied their trade on practically every corner, sometimes hollering vulgarities to get potential customers' attention.

Developing a headache from all the sensorial racket, I ducked into a bar to order a mocktail. No sense getting dehydrated.

"What are you, some kind of missionary?" a male voice said behind me. I spun around on the bar stool and spotted a human in his early twenties with shaggy, sandy blond hair, seated at a table in the back corner of the room. We smiled from mutual recognition, and that little inside joke.

"Piper," I said, bringing my drink to his table. The first time I met him, when he was a stowaway on my ship, he was a freelance shuttle stop hooker with an oversized leather jacket and an undersized T-shirt. Now, he wore the dark blue uniform of an Interstellar One merchant ship crewmember. Apparently, my chance acquaintance had gone up in the world. *Thank you, God, that he got out of prostitution. Now that he's gone legitimate, I wonder if he's going by his real name, Logan Voyle.*

"I never expected to see you here," I said. "It looks like you've gotten yourself fixed up with a merchant ship. Are you on shore leave?"

"Yeah, man," he said, as though we were old friends who picked up a conversation from yesterday. "I've got a week before I have to go back. I'm under contract for two years." There was more than a hint of bitterness in that last statement. No wonder, considering that Piper was used to being self-employed.

"Yeah, two-year contracts tend to be pretty standard with Interstellar One. At least, that's what I've heard. So, what have they got you doing on board?"

Piper scoffed. "What do you think?" He indicated toward his legs, which I hadn't seen because they were tucked under the table. Once I saw the unisex dark blue skirt with its matching easy-open side clasp, my heart sank. Piper hadn't left the life; he was in it worse.

"Piper, I'm so sorry. I didn't know."

"Well, you know now."

"But why, man? I thought you were going to return to your home on Planet Korvathon, get back in touch with your family."

"I did. But then my mom got sick and the medical bills piled up. And my sister needed money for school to continue her studies so she didn't end up hooking like me or married to some stupid jerk who only knows how to scratch his butt and yell for a beer. Didn't I tell you that the only plentiful thing on Korvathon is the poverty? There was no chance of raising enough money for our needs there. So, I signed up with one of Interstellar One's subsidiary merchant ships, *Soaring Raptor*, as a comfort officer to pay my family's bills."

I felt a little sick to my stomach, and not just from the Port Songroi humidity. "Why didn't you call me? I said I would give you help if you needed it."

"Because I'm not a charity case, okay?"

"No, of course not, but a contracted ship prostitute?" I may have been raised in a Christian home, but that didn't make me naïve. Almost everyone knew about the general nature of ship prostitution. It wasn't like brothels or streetwalking, which were bad enough. Ship prostitutes or "comfort officers" signed up for a two-year term to service the whole crew during long sea or space voyages. Away from port, what recourse did they have?

Piper shrugged and knocked back his drink. "It's not like freelancing, that's for sure. When I bumped around from shuttle stop to shuttle stop, I had to dodge vice cops and muggers, but at least I had more control." He snapped to get a waiter's attention. "Bring me a tin of nickies?"

The tentacled alien waiter nodded and then left to retrieve some nicotine chewing gum. Once the waiter was out of earshot, Piper said,

"But when I'm on duty aboard the *Soaring Raptor*, I've got to be open for business if a crewmember needs relief." Sweeping his hand toward his thigh, he added, "Why do you think we're required to wear this getup? Quick and easy access. You know what they say about comfort officers: 'Going commando is mando.'"

I forced myself to gulp down some of my mocktail, as though doing so could settle my stomach.

"Thanks, kiddo," Piper said when the waiter returned with the requested tin of gum. He wasted no time chewing a piece. "Want a nickie?"

"No thanks."

"Oh, that's right. You don't do nicotine. You're a good old church boy." There was no malice in his statement, more like weary resignation. "No drugs, no sex, wearing underpants… Well, maybe you're on to something." Piper grabbed my arm and pulled me close, taking me into his confidence. "Between you and me, Henry, it's a bit of a grind—two three-hour shifts per day, every day. Sure, we've got mandated fifteen-minute hygiene breaks in between throws, and a one-hour break between shifts. But I'm pretty popular, so we're talking an average of ten to twelve crewmembers per day having fun opening the lower half of my uniform. Don't get me started on the ship's prostitution liaison. I mean, he's a cool dude and all, but it can get kind of skeevy when the guy you're supposed to report any concerns to is also the guy in charge of making sure you perform your duties. Plus, he can swing by for a midnight snack whenever he wants, same as any other crewmember."

Oh, God, I thought, my stomach churning, *please find a way for Piper to get out of this wretched life! At least make him* want *to leave.*

Leaning forward, Piper whispered, "Contract or not, I want out."

Unfortunately, God sometimes has a habit of answering prayers a little too fast.

My chest tightened. The brochure that border agent gave me was frighteningly clear about the penalties for transporting a registered prostitute or comfort officer off planet. Breaking a spaceship contract operating under interstellar law was no joke either. But neither one of those threats was going to stop me, even though my legs trembled from what I was about to propose. Once I made my offer, there would be no going back. I steeled myself and stalled for time with another sip of my drink. It burned my throat going down.

"Then that's what we'll do," I said, barely able to get the words out.

"Do what?"

"We're going to leave this hellhole. Tonight." *Congratulations, Henry, you've just announced your intention to break the law on an alien planet. May God protect me, protect us.*

"Henry, are you nuts? You could be charged with aiding and abetting desertion, transportation of a registered comfort officer off planet, and trafficking."

The reality of my wild plan sunk in, turning my breath cold. "Yeah, I could be arrested. So could you. But do you really want to serve out the rest of your contract? I mean, you're logging two three-hour shifts per day with an average of ten to twelve, um, sessions. No offense, but it sounds like you're being treated like a living sex doll."

"You're worried about *me* being treated like a living sex doll? If you get caught trying to help me escape, *you* could end up being treated like a living sex doll—in Port Songroi Jail."

My breaths grew shallow, more from fear than taking offense. If the sleazy atmosphere of Port Songroi's streets was any indication, their penal system was bound to be far worse. "Then we better not get caught."

Piper nodded and then expelled a heavy breath from his nose. "Okay. What's your plan?"

"I… don't have one yet. Not the details, anyway. But I have a ship with a cargo hold, and maybe we could get one of those anti-detector devices from the black market to hide your life signs and biosignature so no one will know that you're on board."

Piper ran his hand through his hair. "That's an idea, but it's a bit risky. If your cargo gets inspected—and I get discovered all wrapped up in a box like a birthday present—we're screwed."

"How common are cargo hold inspections when exiting Port Songroi?"

"For a young, single guy like you, pretty common. Sorry, but the fact that you're a petite, long-haired spice magnate wearing a tropical floral silk shirt screams, 'I'm a sex tourist who isn't above exporting a hooker for a good time back home, 'cause I can afford it and can't get laid without paying for it. Plus, I'm probably transporting a stash of drugs.' No offense; it's just how these border guys operate."

"As unflattering as your description is, you may have a point about how Port Songroi customs authorities profile certain types of tourists and businessmen." The fact a border guard asked me about STD testing and birth control upon entry was evidence enough of government workers' nosiness around here. Any official asking questions like that would have no qualms about poking around in my cargo hold to find hidden prostitutes. I finished my drink, trying to think of a workaround. After a while, vague ideas started forming into a semi-plausible means of escape.

"I have official company business at Prosperity Bottling Company the day after tomorrow," I said, thinking aloud. "They've been sending us defective glass spice containers that have arrived broken, and I'm trying to figure out why. I listed this as my official reason for travel to Port Songroi."

"Yeah, so?"

Think, Henry, think! How can we use this to our advantage? "So, maybe it would be easier to sneak you out in plain sight as an employee of the bottle factory who needs to come back with me to Trevalu Intergalactic Spice Company for an in-person consultation with quality control." *Seriously, Henry? That's the best you can come up with?*

Piper chewed on his nicotine gum for several seconds before responding. "I have a friend in Port Songroi, a gal who can forge electronic documents and make it look like I really work for this bottling company you're talking about."

"You really think my idea sounds possible?"

"Sure, but if a port official calls the company to ask if I really work for them, we're done for."

Right, there's always a potential snag. "Is that standard practice on this planet? To verify the identities of people who are leaving?"

"It depends. Since you arrived at Port Songroi alone, you're definitely going to be questioned if you have a passenger during departure."

I ordered some seltzer water to settle my stomach. Among our escape plans, the humidity, and whatever was in the mocktail I drank earlier, I wasn't feeling so good. Piper ordered himself a glass of chammok, that beverage I saw advertised all over the place on the way to this dive.

"You okay, man? You're looking a little washed out."

"I think it's the heat." I pulled my bandana out of my pocket and dipped it into the seltzer water to wet my neck, trying to cool down.

"Hey, isn't that the bandana I gave you?"

"Yeah, it comes in handy for stuff."

The corners of Piper's lips twitched, like he wanted to smile but couldn't bring himself to do it. Who knows? Maybe he was touched that I kept the thing.

"Back on Korvathon, my sister commandeered the sweater that you gave me." This time, he did smile a little. "You know, that one you knitted for your retreat and sewed that Green Scapular thing inside of it? Protection from your Mother Mary, or some such thing? Anyway, I told her, 'Nina, that's a man's sweater.' And she was like, 'No, it's unisex. Besides, I need to look nice when I apply for a scholarship. No one will know the difference. Even if it doesn't fit quite right, at least it has *style*.'" Piper laughed through his nose a little and then sighed. "Well, she kind of had a point. There are only so many need-based slots, and she wanted to look presentable. Unfortunately, she didn't get chosen. And like I said before, there was no way Mama and I could afford to send her to learn how to become an AI engineer. If she didn't get into school this year, she'd probably end up minding robots at a fuel station for minimum wage, hooking, or marrying some putz with no future. Add that to Mama's medical bills and our congress's recent public assistance cuts… Well, something had to give.

"Anyway, when some comfort officer recruiter showed up at the convenience store where I was working, I didn't hesitate to sign up. I told him, 'As long as my mother and sister don't find out that I've signed on as a whore, you've got yourself a deal.' Yeah, my family thinks that I'm some kind of yeoman or something. But with the high wages I'm sending home for their living expenses and Nina's school tuition, they probably suspect that I'm back in the game. Sorry, I'm rambling."

Piper slugged down some of his chammok.

"No, don't be sorry." Although I probably should have been more concerned about Piper's mental state given all of his hardships, something else occupied my thoughts: "You just gave me an idea of how we can pull off an escape."

"Yeah?"

"When you said your sister wanted to study AI engineering, it got me thinking. If you can get the fake documents you need from that friend of yours, maybe I can set up an AI secretary program on my phone in case port authorities call to check if you're really a quality control inspector from Prosperity Bottling Company. Once you have a fake name for me to enter, I could route the telephone number to my fake secretary, who can say things like, 'Why, yes. We are expecting Mr. So-and-so.' Since the number would be routed through Trevalu Intergalactic Spice Company, it would look and sound legitimate."

For the first time since Piper spotted me at the bar, an energetic light entered his eyes. "I like the way you think. We can't leave tonight though. I need to get in touch with Tchaniki about those documents and get myself some clothes that make me look like a quality control inspector. And don't worry. I'm not fitted with a tracking device or anything, and I used a fake name aboard the *Soaring Raptor*. So, once we get off planet, we're pretty much in the clear."

I nodded, feeling increasingly confident about our escape plan. Even my churning stomach quit bothering me. "Right, and I'm supposed to meet with the head of Prosperity Bottling Company the day after tomorrow, so no chance of leaving tonight anyway without raising suspicion. Tomorrow, I can set up our AI secretary. We may not even need it, but it'll be a backup in case our story gets checked on."

"In the meantime, we shouldn't be seen together."

"Good thinking. My ship is parked in Hangar 5. Can you meet me there the day after tomorrow at 2100 Hours Interstellar Standard Time? That should give us both enough time to get things settled. Then, I can enter whatever fake name your friend gives you into the AI program before we take off."

"Yeah, I'll be there. You're still flying the *Rust Bucket*?"

"Not this trip. I figured it wouldn't be a good idea to fly a ship called the *Rust Bucket* while on official company business. Look for the *Cyclone Thunder*."

"And that's a better ship name for doing business?"

Maybe it was from nervousness, but I couldn't help laughing. Piper joined in.

"All right," Piper said. "I'll see you in Hangar 5, day after tomorrow, at 2100 Hours. Don't worry. I'll be dressed for the part with proper e-documentation."

"Excellent. Until then, God keep you."

I LEFT THE BAR, STILL FEELING A LITTLE QUEASY. AT LEAST IT WAS LATE ENOUGH in the day that I could check into my hotel room down the street and rest for a while. Lying in bed, I prayed a Rosary of the Joyful Mysteries with the petition that Piper and I would escape without incident. If we failed… *Well, God spare us that.*

When I looked out the window a few minutes later, I saw Piper talking to a huge, muscular alien with dark green skin. As they walked toward the old dock together, the alien wrapped his arm around Piper's waist. Ethical issues of prostitution notwithstanding, a man that big could literally break him. But I couldn't risk interfering, doing anything that could jeopardize our escape the day after tomorrow. So, after saying a quick prayer that Piper would stay safe, I opened a program on my watch and got to work creating that AI secretary.

AT THE APPOINTED TIME AND DATE, PIPER MET ME IN HANGAR 5. AT FIRST, I didn't recognize him. His hair was dark brown and he wore a pastel leisure suit, making him look just shabby enough to pass for the kind of mildly interested employee of a hack corporation like Prosperity Bottling Company. When I spoke with the lackadaisical head of the company earlier in the day, it was no surprise that Trevalu Intergalactic Spice Company received two defective shipments in a row. It turned out that the cheap packing material they used from Planet Asiroton caused a breakdown of the glass's chemical components, making the containers shatter en route. That alone wouldn't have been cause for concern. Mistakes like that could be easily rectified. It was the boss's flippant attitude about the damaged goods that bothered me ("So, did you, like, want a refund, man, or something?"). And

I swear the guy was high on something. Yeah, after seeing the company's culture firsthand, Piper's disguise was one hundred percent believable.

"I'm Gordy Holland," Piper said, shaking my hand. *That's a smart move to stay in character in case anybody's watching. The name fits too.*

"Henry Trevalu," I said. "Let me show you around *Cyclone Thunder*." Once we were inside my ship, we could drop the act for a few minutes. I uploaded the name "Gordy Holland" to the secretary program on my watch and tested it several times.

"Hopefully, this will convince the border agent," I said, "but I'm not taking any chances." I took my Rosary out of my pocket.

"Seriously?" Piper raised his eyebrow. "You think that's going to help?"

"Mama Mary's never failed me yet." Although this time, my faith faltered. Like Piper said, if we got caught, it would mean prison for both of us. Even more horrifying, Piper could be ordered back to the *Soaring Raptor* to serve out the rest of his contract—possibly in the brig. *Please, Mother Mary, don't refuse to intercede when it counts.*

To Piper's credit, he kept quiet while I prayed, even though the Sorrowful Mysteries took more than fifteen minutes to recite.

"Ready?" I asked him when I put away my Rosary. My heart crept into my throat, threatening to choke me.

"Ready."

Once cleared for takeoff, I flew straight for the port of exit. Since most of the traffic was incoming for Fleet Week, we arrived within minutes and there wasn't a line. *Please, God, don't let the border agent question us.* I uploaded my e-documents and Piper uploaded his fake ones. The agent scrutinized them.

"Mr. Trevalu," he said, scrolling through my e-papers, "it says here your planned length of stay is two weeks. You've only been here three days."

Crap, I didn't account for that! Whatever you do, Henry, stay calm. Lord, please let us pass!

"There's been a change of plans," I said. The agent waited to hear more. He obviously wasn't going to let us through without a specific explanation. *If only I could think of one…*

"Look, officer," Piper said, rescuing me from my brain block, "we've been trying to handle some shipping supply problems here in Port Songroi, so we did some research, and it turns out that we have to head over to Planète Bonne Chance to track down the origin point of some damaged goods we received. It's one big, tangled, interplanetary mess, and we'd like to solve it as soon as possible."

"Shipping supply problems?" the agent said with a hint of disgust. My chest and stomach clenched. If he tried to detain us, I could make a break for it. Living as fugitives until reaching a sanctuary planet wouldn't be ideal, but I couldn't in good conscience let Piper be hauled away to keep suffering what used to be called a fate worse than death. And frankly, I didn't like the idea of doing time in a Port Songroi penitentiary either. *Please, God, give me the courage to run if needed.*

"Believe me, I know all about shipping problems," the agent continued. "A few months ago, my wife ordered new curtains for our bathtub, but the order got stuck in the company's computer system somehow, so identical curtains started showing up at our door once per week for over a month until the problem got solved—*seven* shipments of curtains in all. So, you gentlemen better hurry up and fix whatever problem your company is going through to save customers aggravation."

"I'm really sorry to hear that," Piper said, his voice calm and soothing. "That's why Henry and I have to leave Port Songroi now instead of in a couple of weeks, to get things straightened out in a timely fashion."

"See that you do. My wife's been threatening to turn the extra bathtub curtains into clothes for the kids. Do you think I want my kids dressed in bathtub curtains like Korvathonian trash?"

"As my colleague said, we'll do our best to rectify our company's supply issues as soon as possible, sir," I said quickly, praying that Piper kept his cool long enough to get out of port.

The agent gave us a curt nod and waved us through. Piper and I didn't speak until entering deep space, where Planet Kuntobahn's laws no longer applied. We weren't totally safe yet, but we passed the worst of the danger. *Thank you, Jesus.*

"Are you okay, man?" I said, not really sure if I should address the agent's nasty remark about Korvathonians or not.

"Yeah, I'm okay," Piper said, smiling. "More than okay. We actually got away with sneaking me off planet. Maybe you were on to something with that prayer bead business."

"Well, the Rosary is a powerful spiritual weapon. No question." I placed my Rosary on the dashboard, so I wouldn't feel the lumpy texture in my pocket while navigating. "But I meant are you okay after what that agent said about Korvathon? That was cruel."

Piper shrugged. "What do you want me to do, Henry? Cry into a beer over it? Yeah, it hurts, but I'll live." He looked out the window for a while. I switched over to autopilot and entered coordinates for Planète Bonne Chance so we could refuel on the way home.

"Man, this fugitive business has me starving." Piper headed for the galley. Since the autopilot was working fine, I decided to join him.

"You know," Piper said while rummaging through my cupboards, "for a guy who just broke the law to help a ship's prostitute go AWOL, you're not a very savvy consumer."

"What do you mean?"

"I mean that pretty much every packaged item in your galley comes from merchant ships that hire contracted comfort officers like me." He read a few labels. "Corabell Tuna. That's produced by Many Waters Seafood Company, a subsidiary of Galactic Ocean Enterprises. Those guys have a huge fleet chock-full of whores. I know because when I was off duty, I got to talk to Sarah, who used to work on one of their vessels. She said that the conditions made sex trafficking look almost wholesome. And here's Mimi's Mac 'n' Cheese. That one's not as obvious because they don't own their own vessels but hire private contractors. So, some of their ships have prostitutes, and others don't. Oh, and this bar of soap on your sink is from Nopala Company. Their ships are considered better than some of their competitors,' but they still enforce standard two-year prostitution contracts. I could go on, but I think you get the idea. The point is, you've got to get with the program and stop buying this crap."

I should have been horrified by the revelation that my galley was filled with products fueled by human and alien suffering, but I was actually kind of ticked off. I mean, I just saved Piper at great personal risk, and he was telling me what to do? Acting like I was a horrible person for having items in my cupboards that ninety-some percent of humans had? *Judging* me?

"Piper," I said, trying to be reasonable, "I believe that prostitution, especially ship prostitution, is a moral evil. But I'm not endorsing prostitution when I buy products that may have unethical practices folded into their faulty supply chains. I mean, it's not like I'm buying things to *specifically* support hiring comfort officers. Think of it this way: Catholics are against using condoms, but that doesn't mean we boycott every store that sells them. That would be impossible because pretty much every store does."

Piper stared at me with his hands on his hips. "That is not the same thing, dude. If you go into a store and you feel that way, you just don't buy condoms. Problem solved. But when you buy something that's made or transported by a company that hires comfort officers, you are *choosing* to financially support their whole operation, not just the parts you find moral or decent."

"Oh, come on, man! Ship prostitution is so deeply embedded into so many industries that nobody would be able to buy anything anymore."

"That's not true, man. And you're not one to talk about availability of resources. You have enough money to buy anything you want. You just have to be willing to be more conscientious about your purchases. That's all."

"No, that's not all," I said, grabbing an apple sauce pouch. Maybe I would be less cranky and make better arguments after eating a snack. "The sad fact is, there are a lot of bad business practices in the universe. Do you have any idea what would be involved to root them all out? You're expecting me to do the impossible."

"Impossible?" Piper gave me what could only be described as the stink eye while I sucked the apple sauce out of its pouch. "That apple sauce you're eating was packaged by Whole Orchard Corporation, a subsidiary of Interstellar One. So, whenever you shove that yummy treat into your mouth, you just remember what was shoved into *my* mouth in order for you to get it."

I opened my mouth to protest, to tell Piper he was being rude, crude, ungrateful, meanspirited, and a whole host of other nasty, well-deserved adjectives, but Piper held up his hand.

"Stop, Henry." The softness of his voice actually scared me a little. "Don't say anything." Piper walked away and returned with my Rosary. I prepared to tell him how out of line he was to touch a sacramental without my permission. But again, he held up his hand. Why his gesture managed to keep me silent, I'll never know. Then, he pressed my Rosary into my palm and squeezed my fingers around it.

"If this aided our escape, then maybe it can help you think about what I've said."

I STUMBLED OFF TO MY CABIN IN A DAZE, CLUTCHING THE ROSARY. KNEELING beside my bed, I gritted my teeth through the First and Second Glorious Mysteries. Piper had a *lot* of nerve to turn my faith against me like this. But I was going to pray for him anyway because that was the Christian thing to do—to ask God to bless insufferable people. By the Third Glorious Mystery, I calmed down. During the Fourth Glorious Mystery, my mind replayed everything Piper said to me about the products in my cupboards. The Fifth Glorious Mystery left me begging for forgiveness for my sins. After the Hail Holy Queen, I lay down in bed to mull things over.

"Piper?" I said, returning to the galley after a period of reflection. Piper was helping himself to some leftover breaded chicken tenders and broccoli that I had in the freezer. He must have microwaved them while I was in my cabin.

"Yeah?"

"I'm sorry."

Piper nudged his plate and a spare fork in my direction, inviting me to share. I took him up on his offer, not bothering to get my own plate.

"I'm sorry too," Piper said after a long silence. "I shouldn't have railed on you like that, certainly not after what you did for me."

Warmth filled my chest. "Yeah, well, maybe I needed to be railed on a little bit. And thanks for shoving my Rosary into my hand. I needed that too."

"You're welcome, I guess."

"And I'm going to take your… advice to stop buying products with prostitution in the ranks. Like you said, I can afford to make better choices."

"I'm… glad to hear that."

I was getting pretty hungry, so I quit eating off of Piper's plate and brought out some more chicken tenders and broccoli for both of us. While they cooked in the microwave, I put out a full place setting for myself and made tea for Piper and me.

"I've been thinking," I said while we ate and drank. "You're right about how insidious and ingrained ship prostitution is in the supply chain of most major corporations. And"—I looked at my plate, ashamed to meet Piper's eyes—"Trevalu Intergalactic Spice Company needs to become more selective with our suppliers too." I looked at Piper, forgetting my shame out of a need to offer clarification. "Please don't misunderstand. I mean, we certainly don't have any comfort officers on our own cargo vessels. My parents and I have been against that from the beginning on account of our faith—and just plain common decency. But-" I swallowed a bite of broccoli, trying to give myself some time to think about how to follow up on that "but."

"But there are ship prostitutes in your company's supply chain down the line, aren't there?" The gentleness of Piper's voice hurt worse than a shrill accusation would have. I swallowed and nodded. It was really hard to keep my eyes on Piper's face after that admission, but I forced myself.

"Yeah. I guess there came a point where we became so far removed from it, that we turned a blind eye. As long as it wasn't happening on *our* ships, what other people did on *their* ships with consenting adults was *their* business, *their* problem. But that *is* our problem, no matter how far away those ships are from headquarters."

There was another silence, but it wasn't a pleasant one. It forced me to sit with my guilt, and it felt really, really gross—just as it should have.

"So, what are you going to do about it?"

That was the exact question I had been asking myself after reciting the Glorious Mysteries. "Actually," I said, praying that my idea would bear good fruit, "I was hoping you might consider letting me hire you as the manager of supply chain ethics, a division I want to create at Trevalu Intergalactic Spice Company."

"You want to hire me?" Piper's tone bordered on skeptical.

"Piper, you know the business of ship prostitution from stem to stern—literally. The fact that you could pull all of those products out of my cupboards and know exactly where they came from and what conditions the comfort officers faced on the cargo ships run by different companies off the top of your head… I could use your expertise for cleaning up the hidden filth in our supply lines. What do you say?"

"I don't know. It depends on if you want to make real change or just sweep systemic problems under the rug."

Humility is a Christian virtue. So, I swallowed my instinct to argue and asked, "What would you suggest?"

"Okay, well, first of all, I'm glad you're going to be a more attentive consumer. And I think that you have a good idea to eliminate ship prostitution from your supply chain, no matter how tangentially linked. But then what? I mean, people don't sign up to be comfort officers because they have a college education and a trust fund. Look at me. Do you think I would have agreed to turn tricks for roughly six hours a day, every day, locked into a two-year contract, with no choice of clients if I had better options?"

"No, of course not."

"Right. So, if you simply boycott companies that hire comfort officers—even though that's a good start—the prostitutes' lives don't magically get better. We still have bills to pay and families to care for, and most of us aren't getting job offers to become supply chain ethics managers. So, you've got to think long term—education, gainful employment, stuff like that. And by the way, working to outlaw ship prostitution is a really bad idea. That just ends up moving prostitutes from one cage to another, giving them criminal records that make upward mobility even harder. I'm not in favor of legally punishing clients either. A lot of them are pretty decent people wrapped up in a bad system. If you want them to stop using prostitutes' services, show them the harm they're causing, but don't add to that harm by throwing them into the slammer."

I nodded, letting Piper take the lead. So far, his proposals made a lot of sense.

"And I also think it would be a good idea to create a new industry standard for labeling products—with Trevalu Intergalactic Spice Company leading the way. Think about it. You know how sometimes you pick up a product at the store and it says it's vegan or doesn't contain GMOs or was produced in compliance with certain wage and safety standards? We ought to create a label for prostitution-free products. Then, other companies could be encouraged to follow suit by our example. I'm thinking that the official label for prostitution-free products could be a simple cartoon drawing of a man and a woman standing side by side, wearing comfort officer uniforms, crossing their arms in front of their skirts as though saying, 'no access.'"

"That's… actually pretty genius. I like it."

"Isn't it though?" Piper leaned forward, quite animated. "Also, comfort officers who leave before fulfilling their contracts need refuge on sanctuary planets and free legal assistance to prevent bounty hunters from forcing them to return to their ships. And in case you're wondering, you don't have to worry about me in that regard. Like I said, I signed on to the *Soaring Raptor* under a false identity. Of course, if they *do* come looking for me, I'll expect you to put your money to good use for my legal defense. Or just bribe 'em. After all, you can afford it."

"You know I won't let you get dragged back to *Soaring Raptor*. No way."

Piper chuckled. "Well, you better not because that would be pretty bad PR if contract enforcers pursued Logan Voyle, manager of supply chain ethics at Trevalu Intergalactic Spice Company." He grinned, and so did I.

"So, you accept?"

"As long as you give me an obscenely high salary and free rein to do as I see fit to help eliminate the centuries' old practice of contracted ship prostitution, you have yourself a deal." He stuck out his hand.

Letting a straight talking, former comfort officer have free rein over an entire division of Trevalu Intergalactic Spice Company for ridiculously high pay sounded crazy in the best possible way. I shook his hand. "It's a deal."

The End

THE SERPENT, THE DOVE, AND THE SOARING RAPTOR

[EPISODE 9]

As soon as I ended my business call with Stellacross Enterprises, two government goons wearing dark suits burst into my office. One was human and the other was a pale green gelatinous alien approximating the shape of a human. Both of them whipped out their badges. My therapy sanchat, Gabrielle, who had been playing with the pens on my desk, arched her back and hissed. Her wings and tail stiffened with irritation. She narrowed her huge anime eyes at the intruders in warning.

"Henry Trevalu," the human said, still flashing his badge, "I'm Agent Burke, and this is Agent Givordox. We're from the Interstellar Investigation Commission." He and Givordox pocketed their badges in sync, equally expressionless. If I weren't afraid of being hauled off to prison, I would have told them they missed their calling as precision dancers. Too bad they were too tall to qualify for the Marvelous Min Pins Precision Dance Troupe.

"What are you doing in my office?" I had more than an inkling about why these two entered Trevalu Intergalactic Spice Company headquarters, but I had to put up a brave front. If there was ever a time to flaunt the wealth and privilege of being the sole heir and fifty percent owner of the family business, this was it. Gabrielle perched on my shoulder, leaned forward, and hissed at the agents again, daring them to take one step closer.

"I think you know why we're here, Mr. Trevalu," Burke said.

Now, I was certain about the reason for their visit, but I would never admit to the so-called crime. Even though my heart beat louder than a Neon Spark Plug drum solo, I pressed the security button under my desk.

"You gentlemen have about two minutes to leave my office before security arrives." My throat went dry and my legs trembled. I sat down on my important-looking, cushioned swivel chair, trying to play it cool. To steady my nerves and look blasé, I gently peeled Gabrielle from my shoulder to pet her on my lap. My goal was to give the impression of some movie gangster staring down the feds even though they towered over him. Inside, though, I was praying, *Jesus, Mary, and Joseph, please don't let me get extradited to Port Songroi!* Thank goodness the desk hid my bouncing knees—sort of.

Givordox reached into his jacket pocket. I froze, unable to formulate a coherent internal prayer that I wasn't about to get my brains blown out. Not that Interstellar Investigation Commission agents were known for doing that, but after everything I had endured in the past year, my trust in the authorities was nil. When he pulled out a portable holographic plate instead of a weapon, I barely held back a sigh of relief.

While Givordox booted up the plate on my desk, Burke said, "We have good reason to believe Trevalu Intergalactic Spice Company is aiding, abetting, harboring, and hiring a fugitive comfort officer who deserted the Interstellar One merchant ship *Soaring Raptor*." A high-definition, full-color digital tabloid newspaper article hovered above the holographic plate. The headline read, "RUNAWAY SPACE HOOKER HEADS ETHICS DIVISION OF CATHOLIC COMPANY."

Below the headline's blocky letters were two side-by-side photographs. The professional photograph on the right was indeed Trevalu Intergalactic Spice Company's manager of supply chain ethics, Logan Voyle, dressed in a dark green brocade suit while seated at his desk. The less polished, older photograph on the left showed the same man dressed in his comfort officer uniform, including the short unisex skirt with easy-open side clasps. He was dancing in a sleezy bar across from a huge muscular alien decked out in some black leather getup. A pink neon sign above Logan and the alien read "Pleasure Port." Both photos were credited to freelance photographer Coccinelle "Coaxie" Royer. I willed myself not to swallow from nervousness and anger. Shutterbug Coaxie didn't care whose lives she ruined as long as her photos got published.

"If you don't cooperate with us," Burke said, "you're looking at three years behind bars on Planet Kuntobahn in addition to a 500,000 bayvan fine. That's about 250,000 universal credits, to put things into perspective."

I said nothing, praying that Mr. Flubby would show up soon to escort these guys out of my office, out of Trevalu Intergalactic Spice Company headquarters, and hopefully off-planet. (Yes, my Burbalok head of security is actually named Mr. Flubby. It probably sounds intimidating in his native language, but in English, it's hard not to laugh.) Gabrielle curled her tail around my wrist and stared at the agents. Her wings expanded slightly, like she was ready to pounce. Givordox's cheek twitched, but that was the closest he came to showing emotion.

"Mr. Trevalu, I'm going to be blunt," Burke said. "You're only twenty-two years old and, by all accounts, extremely wealthy. You have a lot to lose by not cooperating with the authorities. The maximum 500,000 bayvan fine may not mean much to you, but Port Songroi Jail is no place for a petite, pampered spice magnate like you. We're talking poor, primitive conditions—overcrowding, bad food, filth, violence. And you're not naïve. I don't need to spell out what kind of violence you'd likely be subjected to from prisoners with loose morals and no creature comforts."

I tried to pray a Hail Mary in my head to keep myself from blurting out something incriminating, but the words got jumbled in my brain. *And why hasn't Flubby answered my security call yet?*

"However, if you hand over Logan Voyle, the Interstellar Investigation Commission is willing to overlook your role in this—just a little fine, no prison time. After all, it's quite easy to assume that your transporting the man off-planet was an entirely innocent, unfortunate mistake. Unless, of course, you refuse to cooperate. In which case, we'll have to assume you deliberately aided Mr. Voyle in his desertion."

These creeps want me to betray Logan so he can be dragged back to the Soaring Raptor *in chains? So, he can keep being prostituted until his two-year contract is up? And if I don't rat on him, I'm going to Port Songroi Jail?* My stomach roiled, and yet I had never been happier to break an unjust law. Still, the prospect of incarceration on an alien planet was nothing to sneeze at. Been there, done that. And during my last foray inside an alien prison, I wound up pregnant with two thousand tiny Uhumbra fry. (It's a long story; don't ask.) No thank you to repeating that experience or anything like it. Gabrielle must have sensed my turmoil and climbed up to my shoulder again, attempting to ground me.

"Have you nothing to say for yourself?" Givordox's voice startled me, as he hadn't made a sound until that point. He spoke Universal I fine, but his enunciation could only be described as a bizarre cross between grinding gravel and popping bubbles. Then again, his vocalizations were oddly fitting for someone who looked like an oversized gelatin sculpture. He returned the holographic plate to his pocket, keeping his eyes on me. Burke glanced in his fellow agent's direction and then zeroed in on me.

"Yes, I have something to say." I couldn't help clearing my throat. The combination of fear and indignation sounded way too much like a teenager's voice cracking. "My head of security is entering this room within the next minute to show you out." *Although Flubby literally throwing you out and delivering a solid kick in the rear would be more appropriate. Not Christian, but appropriate.*

"If you have nothing to hide, you shouldn't have any problems with our conducting a search of your business."

That was such lazy, typical, authoritarian claptrap, and I wasn't falling for it.

"Unless you have a search warrant, you're trespassing. Get out."

The next time Burke opened his mouth, Flubby ducked under the doorway to enter the room. He was broader than Burke and Givordox combined, and his head nearly touched the ceiling. For his species though, his size was merely average. If my heart and head weren't pounding with adrenaline, I would have smirked at the agents, both of whom visibly paled a shade.

"Mr. Flubby,"—too bad I had to clear my throat again to get my words out—"these are Agents Burke and Givordox from the Interstellar Investigation Commission. Please see that they are safely escorted out of the building and stay out."

Flubby, who I suspected had his own negative encounters with the law, grinned. "With pleasure, Mr. Trevalu." He cracked his pinkish purple knuckles and grabbed the agents by their elbows. "This way, *gentlemen.*"

"We'll be back with a warrant, Mr. Trevalu," Burke said with eerie calmness as Flubby hauled him and his partner out of the room. "I guarantee it."

If Flubby or the agents said anything in the hallway after that, I didn't hear them. Now that the immediate danger passed, my heart slammed against my eardrums. Gabrielle placed one hand on my chest, curled her tail against my back, and gently flapped her wings, reminding me to breathe.

"Thanks, Gabrielle, but I'm not having a flashback." I scratched her behind the ears, letting her know that I was firmly in reality. Although I definitely wasn't okay. "Come on, girl. We've got to talk to Ms. Mendoza before those thugs come back."

Gabrielle trilled and flapped. In that one-sided exchange, she probably only understood the words "Ms. Mendoza," who kept a basket of toys to keep children busy during their adults' legal appointments. It never occurred to Gabrielle that the plush animals, wooden blocks, silk scarves, rattles, and fashion dolls had a purpose outside of being her own personal treasure trove when we came to visit. The fact that Mendoza kept a jar of sugar-free suckers on her desk certainly didn't lower Gabrielle's high opinion of her.

"No candy for you today," I said to distract myself from the dire circumstances. "The last thing I need right now is an extra trip to the-" I stopped myself from saying "vet" or "Dr. Xirvan" just in time. I didn't need a shrieking, fluffy white mutiny on my hands either.

Please, God, don't let her be with a client right now, I prayed as I took the elevator downstairs. Just because Mendoza was on retainer didn't mean she sat at her desk twiddling her thumbs until my parents or I showed up. For all I knew, she could be handling some contract dispute with

Stellacross Enterprises, whose CEO I was on the phone with most of the morning. Ever since Trevalu Intergalactic Spice Company cut ties with any contractors known to hire comfort officers aboard their sea or space vessels, it had been a legal zoo around here. It wouldn't surprise me if some angry merchant ship owner tipped off Coaxie about our manager of supply chain ethics being a runaway ship's prostitute as payback.

Thankfully, Mendoza wasn't with a client or on the phone when I arrived. *Thank you, Jesus.*

"Good afternoon, Mr. Trevalu." She stood when I entered the room. It weirded me out a little. Yeah, as half owner of the company, I was technically one of the bosses, but it was only recently that most of the staff started calling me Mr. Trevalu instead of just Henry and would stand whenever I entered a room. At least Logan didn't tiptoe around me like I was going to fire him if he didn't. But I couldn't worry about protocol right now.

"Hello, Ms. Mendoza." I shook her hand and then sat across from her. Gabrielle, who had no notion of manners whatsoever, jumped from my shoulder and dive bombed the toy basket. "I have a serious legal situation that we need to sort out, pronto."

She raised her eyebrow. "More serious than the situation with Stellacross Enterprises claiming breach of contract for Trevalu Intergalactic Spice Company cancelling their container shipments?"

"Try about a million times more serious. A couple of Interstellar Investigation Commission agents just barged into my office and threatened to have me and Logan Voyle arrested." I took out my red paisley bandana, the one Logan gave me a while back, to wipe the sweat from my neck and forehead.

"Arrested? On what grounds?"

Something squeaked from the toy basket, followed by Gabrielle's playful growl.

"On the grounds that Logan is a runaway ship prostitute, and that I helped him flee during his shore leave at Port Songroi."

"What a slanderous statement! Don't you worry, Mr. Trevalu. Mr. Voyle is a fine, upstanding employee. We'll get this sorted out. By the time

I'm done with this case, no one will even *think* of accusing our supply chain ethics manager of engaging in the very trade he's been fighting against."

"Oh, uh, no! I'm not asking you to sue for slander. It's worse than that. The accusations are true."

Mendoza blinked, her eyes wide. Her lower lip twitched. "Mr. Trevalu," she said, her eyes still bulging with disbelief, "you don't mean to say… You mean, Mr. Voyle is a contracted comfort officer?"

A sigh drained out of me. "Yeah, the jig is up. Take a look at this." I hastily performed an internet search on my watch to find the article the agents showed me on their holographic plate. The headline, photographs, and first paragraph of the article appeared, but the rest of the text was hidden behind a paywall for subscribers only. Still, I made the free portions hover above my watch so Mendoza could see the kind of trouble Logan and I were in.

"Well, I'll be…" Her eyes darted between the two photos. "But… but Mr. Voyle created that prostitution-free label for store products, with our company leading the way toward the abolition of ship prostitution."

"Yeah, that's why Logan's fought so hard to root out ship prostitution among our contractors. He knows how deeply engrained it is in company supply chains, and how awful it is to have to service a whole merchant ship's crew on command. That's why he deserted, and I helped him."

Gabrielle leapt onto the desk with a bedraggled female fashion doll trapped between her teeth. She shook it and growled, like she made a fresh kill.

"Not now, Gabrielle." I put her back on the floor, leaving the poor doll to its fate.

"Mr. Trevalu, while I can appreciate your moral compass and sense of justice, you and Mr. Voyle are looking at serious charges here."

"Tell me about it. No, wait. Don't tell me about it. I already know. What I need from you is some truly masterful legal maneuvering. Like I said, all of the accusations that I'm aware of are true. See, I was handling a company business matter on Planet Kuntobahn when I ran into Logan in Port Songroi. It was just a chance meeting. And while we talked, it came out that since the last time I saw him, he became a comfort officer aboard the Interstellar One merchant spaceship, *Soaring Raptor*. He said that he signed a two-year contract under a false name because his mom was sick and his sister needed money for college, but that it was a terrible grind and he wanted out. I mean, the poor guy was logging ten to twelve… er, *sessions* per day."

"So, you helped him escape from Planet Kuntobahn?"

"Yes, I did."

"Were you aware that helping a contracted comfort officer desert his post is a violation of both interstellar law and the laws of Port Songroi?"

"Yes, I was."

Mendoza pinched the bridge of her nose. "Mr. Trevalu, you obviously can't get out of this by pleading ignorance."

"I don't intend to plead ignorance. I was hoping we could figure out some legal loophole to make this whole situation go away—especially for Logan. Can you believe those agents wanted me to rat him out? Okay, actually, that's pretty believable."

"Rat him out?"

"Yeah, Agent Burke was like, 'if you hand over Logan Voyle, we'll let you off with a small fine and no jail time.' Say, can you nail him on bribery charges or something?"

"Unfortunately, no. The Interstellar Investigation Commission has the authority to offer suspects and prisoners deals like that, to turn them into informants in exchange for reduced charges."

"You mean squealers." I scoffed, but my disgusted noise got overpowered by a rapid series of loud squeaks due to Gabrielle pulverizing a squeaker toy.

"Essentially, yes. Of course, I'll do everything in my power to defend you and Mr. Voyle. In the meantime, do not speak with any authorities unless I'm with you. Tell me, did you admit to any illegal activity in the agents' presence?"

"No, I didn't say anything except that they were trespassing and that security was going to escort them out in two minutes."

"That's good. Don't do anything to incriminate yourself or Mr. Voyle. As long as you don't admit to anything, it will be easier to reduce charges."

The bandana I forgot I had been holding was crumpled into a tight ball in my fist. Its rumpled form somehow made me think of Logan curled up in the corner of *Soaring Raptor's* brig to fulfill the remainder of his contract. I didn't know how much time he had left, but whatever it was, it was too much. Contract or not, indentured sexual servitude was vile. By all the saints and angels, I wasn't going to let my friend get dragged back to that kind of hell ship.

"Ms. Mendoza, I'm afraid that reduced charges aren't enough. I am dead serious that Logan and I need all charges against us dropped. No plea bargaining, no prison time, and Logan remains free. I don't care if I need to settle out of court with a hefty sum that drains half the company's resources, but Logan's not going back to the *Soaring Raptor*, and I'm not going to prison."

Mendoza folded her hands on her desk. Her expression and voice softened. "Surely, you realize I can't promise all that."

I nodded. "I know." *But if we can't settle this legally,* I thought, *I'll help Logan escape again. When it comes to the law of man versus the law of God, I know which to obey.* "It won't be long before those agents return with a search warrant, followed by arrest warrants."

"Indeed. In the meantime, you better stay here at headquarters or at home. Even though you aren't under arrest yet, it wouldn't look good if you left town."

"Fair enough, but what about Logan? I have no idea where he is right now. The last time he checked in with me, he was inspecting the Fort Hollister Distribution Center on Planète Bonne Chance."

"Based on those tabloid photos you showed me, it's possible that he may already be under arrest."

I don't know why that hadn't occurred to me before, but it made my blood freeze in my veins. A few harsh heartbeats unfroze them, but my chest remained tight. "Is there a way you can find out if he's in jail?"

Mendoza slid her desktop computer closer to herself. "I can run a general search." She typed something. Behind me, several objects thumped against the floor, courtesy of Gabrielle. While waiting for the internet search results, I silently prayed the beginning of a Rosary, remembering the words now that interstellar feds weren't threatening me in my office.

"I found something." Mendoza turned her computer toward me. "Logan Voyle, alias: Piper Long, alias: Gordy Holland, currently at large."

"So, they've already secured the warrant for his arrest."

"It sure looks like it." She turned the laptop back toward herself and resumed typing. "If he contacts Trevalu Intergalactic Spice Company, we'll have to convince him to turn himself in."

"What?" Behind me, Gabrielle emitted a startled chirp. I must have been pretty loud. "Ms. Mendoza, if Logan turns himself in, he'll be back on the *Soaring Raptor* within a week! You know how fast those Interstellar One merchant ships operate. And given that one of their captains suffered the embarrassment of a successful desertion, they're going to want to make an example out of Logan."

"Mr. Trevalu, I have just confirmed that Logan is classified as a fugitive in this sector. Any contact with him, other than to convince him to surrender to the authorities, would constitute aiding, abetting, and harboring. That's in addition to the fact that you're already under suspicion on those charges back in Port Songroi. And the evidence against you is pretty damning, your disclosure to me notwithstanding. Of course, you have attorney-client privilege, but that's not going to help you much in the face of solid evidence."

"Ms. Mendoza," I said, trying to keep my voice level, "I must reiterate that if Logan is captured, the odds are extremely high that he'll be returned to the *Soaring Raptor* to fulfill his contract."

"Yes, that's a strong possibility."

"And that doesn't upset you?"

She quit typing and closed her laptop. "It's not a question of being upset. It's a question of legality."

"No, it's a question of *morality*. Look, I know Logan signed a two-year contract to be a comfort officer—out of desperation, I might add—but that doesn't mean allowing the authorities to enforce such a contract is moral."

"I agree with you, but our legal options for fighting this form of immorality are limited."

"I understand. Just… do what you can, please." I stood to leave. "Thank you, Ms. Mendoza." I shook her hand. "I trust you'll do everything in your power to help Logan and me."

"I'll do my best. That much, I can promise."

Before leaving, I put all of the toys Gabrielle scattered over the floor back into the basket. While I cleaned up, Mendoza gave Gabrielle a bag of dried cranberries—with my permission—instead of candy. Gabrielle trilled and purred at the same time as she perched on my shoulder and ate her snack out of the bag, one cranberry at a time. As soon as we left Mendoza's office, I returned to my own with the beginnings of a wild scheme in mind.

It's too dangerous and obvious to call Logan to warn him, I thought as I searched through the contacts stored on my watch. *Agents Burke and Givordox will be expecting that. And I can't just sit around for Mendoza to come up with a convoluted legal solution while Logan may be languishing in a jail cell or aboard the* Soaring Raptor. *No, there's only one person I can call, someone the feds wouldn't think I'd want anything to do with given the circumstances. Ah, found it!* I hit the call button.

"Yello, Coaxie Royer here." Her image hovered over my watch. As usual, a camera was slung over her shoulder. It looked like she was in some dingy apartment with peeling paint on the walls. A pile of papers lay scattered on a nearby table.

"Hey, Coaxie. Those were some revealing pictures you took of Trevalu Intergalactic Spice Company's manager of supply chain ethics for the tabloids." I tried to keep my tone neutral, but it was tough knowing that this little wretch was largely responsible for the Interstellar Investigation Commission's, well, investigation. Gabrielle's tail brushed across my face, so I gently pushed it out of the way. She chittered and then continued eating her cranberries.

"Aw, don't be sore at me. I don't create scandals. I just take pictures of 'em."

"Right." I refrained from telling her that selling incriminating pictures to the press *did* constitute a type of scandal, but if I wanted her help, I couldn't argue. Flattery might get better results, especially considering I was about to propose something borderline illegal. "I have to admit that it's pretty scandalous. Good quality pictures, too. What was the headline again, something like 'Catholic Company Hires Comfort Officer?'"

"No, it was 'Runaway Space Hooker Heads Ethics Division of Catholic Company.' I know because I've got my contributor copy on the kitchen table. But if it makes you feel better, I don't write the headlines or the articles. I just get paid for the pictures."

"Yeah, about that… Listen, did you discover Logan Voyle used to be a comfort officer on your own, or did someone send you to do some investigating?"

"Actually, it was more of a fortunate accident. I took a lot of pictures at Port Songroi during Fleet Week, hoping that some of them would get picked up by the tabloids. I didn't know who that guy dancing in the bar was, but I thought for sure someone would want to buy his picture. It didn't get picked up though, so I held onto it. Then, when I did that photo op of Logan Voyle a couple of weeks ago, I thought he looked familiar. So, I went through my old pictures and BAM! There he was. And I thought, *daaang*, there's a story for the tabloids here. This time, one of 'em picked it up."

"Yeah, well, thanks to your accidental photojournalism, there's a warrant out for Logan's arrest on the grounds of desertion. And I'm in the hot seat too."

"Aw, man. That really sucks for both of you."

"That's putting it mildly."

Gabrielle finished her cranberries, threw the empty bag into the garbage can (I trained her to do that!), and flew to her bed to take a nap. She wrapped herself in the wool baby blanket I knitted for her and fell asleep almost instantly.

"Anyway, I didn't call to harangue you about the tabloids," I said. "Actually, I may have a lucrative proposition for you."

"Yeah?"

"You travel through various social circles for your work. Do you know anything about Agent Burke and Agent Givordox from the Interstellar Investigation Commission?"

Coaxie's face contorted in thought. "Nope. Never heard of 'em. Why?"

"Because those are the two agents who barged into my office this morning trying to shake me down for information about Logan. I was hoping maybe you had some dirt on those two."

"Dirt on IIC agents? I like the sound of that. Lemme guess. You want me to take pictures of them doing something so scandalous that they have to drop the charges against you or face career ruination, amirite?"

Despite the gravity of my situation, I smiled. "I'll neither confirm nor deny that. Neither will I confirm nor deny a hefty bounty upon delivery of said evidence."

She winked. "I gotcha loud 'n' clear. It'll take time though."

"Unfortunately, time is in short supply considering there's already a warrant for Logan's arrest."

"So, you've said. But don't worry too much. I'm guessing Logan's hunkering down on some sanctuary planet."

"I sure hope so. But I can't risk calling him to find out. His communications are probably wiretapped. Mine could be too in a minute, if the IIC secures a warrant."

"Copy that. Just lay low, and I'll do what I can. Agents Burke and Givordox, you said?" She scribbled something on a paper scrap.

"Yeah. Burke's human, but I don't know the species of the other guy. Givordox looks kind of like pale green squishy gelatin molded to look like a human, if that makes sense."

"Pale green squishy gelatin, huh? Sounds like an Alodeon. Quite a conservative culture—in public, anyway. By the way, am I the only person in the galaxy who thinks that 'Alodeon' sounds like a prescription drug you would use to treat toenail fungus? Anyway, I'll see what I can find. When I get the scoop, I might just swing by to do a 'photo op' of the disgraced Henry Trevalu." She put "photo op" in air quotes. My chest tingled at the prospect of this plan actually working. If Coaxie got the goods on our IIC agents, she'd have an excuse to drop by my office without causing suspicion. After all, rich businesspeople often got plagued by photo ops, something I knew firsthand.

"You've got it, Coaxie. Swing by here for that 'photo op' as soon as you find out anything. If they won't let you past the front desk, just make a dash for the elevator. You're a pushy freelance photographer, after all, so I assume you're good at that."

"Hah! You flatter me. Tootles!" Coaxie hung up. As a precaution, I deleted the record of our phone conversation. Then, after pacing for a few tense minutes, I forced myself to sit down and pray a whole fifteen-decade Rosary with the intention that Logan found a safe haven. There was no sense tromping around waiting for Burke and Givordox to show up again, as they surely would. Oblivious to my stress, Gabrielle emitted a single snort in her sleep.

"GOOD HEAVENS, IS LOGAN REALLY A PROSTITUTE?" MOM SAID WHEN SHE called that afternoon. She and Dad were off-planet for a business conference. No doubt they saw the tabloid article. "You told your father and me that he had extensive experience with company ethics."

It wasn't a lie so much as a mental reservation. As a former comfort officer, Logan *did* have extensive experience with company ethics—or lack thereof. When I officially hired him, I just conveniently left out the part that he knew about the plight of comfort officers on merchant ships because he was one.

"Mom, Logan *is* experienced when it comes to company ethics, but I can't talk about this case right now."

"Oh, Henry, please don't let this be a repeat of Zakon-4. Your father and I are worried sick."

"Well, if it makes you feel any better, I seriously doubt this situation will end with my getting pregnant again."

"That is *not* funny, young man. And according to the article I read, transporting a registered comfort officer out of Port Songroi can be punished with up to three years in prison. Did you see that documentary about Port Songroi Jail that just aired on Télétoile? Heaven knows *what* would happen to you in a place like that. Your father's so upset that he had to put sodium bicarbonate in his drink after lunch."

No, I hadn't seen the documentary, and Port Songroi Jail's undoubtedly horrific conditions weren't something I wanted to discuss. Plus, Dad's indigestion was more likely due to the food provided at the conference than a documentary about a penitentiary where I might end up. Then again, he could be sensitive like that. Either way, I didn't need my parents needlessly worrying. "Mom, I've got Ms. Mendoza on the case. Everything'll be fine."

She groaned and sighed at the same time. "Do you want us to come home early?"

"No, that's okay. I'm fine." *Well, sort of fine, I guess. I'm sitting on an invisible pin cushion waiting for those government goobers to show up again. God help me.* "Actually, it's getting close to closing hours, so I better lock everything up before heading home."

"Oh, that's right. I keep forgetting the time zone difference. I'll try not to accidentally call you in the middle of the night. I wouldn't want to interfere with your beauty sleep."

I chuckled at Mom's attempt at levity. "Yeah, I'll see you and Dad next week or so. Bye."

After hanging up, I fussed with some papers in my office and made sure all of my cabinets were locked. As soon as the last employee left, I would go home and make myself some dinner—assuming I could calm down enough to eat.

"Come on, Gabrielle," I said to the winged monkey-cat climbing up the leg of my desk. Later, I would have to add a little jungle gym to the corner of my office. Being the boss came with privileges. With a cheerful trill, she flew onto my shoulder and picked through my hair. Just as I was about to lock the door, my watch phone rang. The caller ID said, "Unknown number, possibly spam."

I should've let the answering machine pick it up, but curiosity got the better of me. "Hello? Henry Trevalu speaking." My watch screen said "call connected," but there was no accompanying image. Whoever called didn't want to be seen.

"Henry, get off-planet *now.* The IIC's on your tail."

My heartrate accelerated. "Logan?"

"Yeah, who did you think it was, the Tooth Fairy? Listen, fly the *Rust Bucket* or *Cyclone Thunder* or whatever you're driving these days to a sanctuary planet while you still can."

"Never mind about me. What about you? Are you safe?"

"Safe enough. I hightailed it for a sanctuary planet the moment I saw that stupid tabloid article. I landed without incident and checked into a cheap motel until things blow over. Don't ask me where I am though. I'm calling you from a burner."

Thank you, Lord. I made a Sign of the Cross in gratitude. As long as Logan stayed on a sanctuary planet, *any* sanctuary planet, he was safe from legal extradition. Of course, *illegal* bounty hunters existed, but they were far less of a threat than the Interstellar Investigation Commission. "Praise be to God."

"Save the praise for later. Word on the street is that the interstellar feds are *this* close to securing a warrant for your arrest. So, you've got to leave *now*."

"I know, but I'm not running." *At least not yet.* "I have a good lawyer."

"I don't care how good your lawyer is. That won't protect you from being arrested. Do you really want to go to jail?"

"Of course, I don't want to go to jail." I locked up my office and headed down the hall. "But I don't want to be on the lam either. Besides, there's got to be a better way out of this."

"Yeah, well, until you find some magical solution, I'm hunkering down. Don't worry. Like I said, I'm using an encrypted burner phone, and the feds can't snatch me anyway. Well, not legally, that is. But I can take care of myself. It's you I'm worried about. You're not exactly a gentleman of the streets."

"I appreciate your concern, but I have a backup plan." *That is, if one considers an abundance of prayer and faith in Coaxie Royer's dubious investigation abilities a backup plan.* But the thought of Coaxie snapping incriminating photographs gave me an idea. "Logan, do you know anything about Agent Burke or Agent Givordox? Best I can tell, they've been assigned to this case. Those well-dressed punks burst into my office this morning wanting me to rat you out for a slap on the wrist. I had Mr. Flubby throw them out."

Logan chuckled. "Too bad you didn't catch that on video."

"Yeah, I know. But Ms. Mendoza says IIC guys are allowed to offer lighter sentences to suspects in exchange for information."

"No, not that. I meant it's too bad you didn't catch on video those punks getting thrown out by Flubby. That sounds hilarious."

The elevator felt unusually slow tonight. "Eh… not really, but focus. Do you know anything at all about those two guys who came into my office, anything that can help us?"

"What were their names again?"

"Burke and Givordox. They didn't give their first names."

I finally arrived downstairs. Normally, being alone at headquarters didn't bother me, but it felt like some thug was going to jump me at any moment. Even the cleaning robots starting their shift creeped me out a little.

"Nope, never heard of them. Of course, those might be aliases. Can you send me their pictures?"

"Ah, good thinking. They should be on the security cameras outside of the building and in the lobby." Gabrielle picked at a loose thread on my collar while I searched through the building's security footage. *Found it!* I sent the videos to Logan. "Does that help?"

"Sorry, I haven't seen those guys. But I'll ask around. The folks around here really don't like interstellar cops—or any cops, for that matter—and for good reason. I'll see what I can dig up. In the meantime, if you're going to stick around at company headquarters, don't call me. It wouldn't look good for me to keep showing up on your phone records."

"Agreed. Stay safe, and God keep you." I hung up and went home, looking over my shoulder several times along the way. Although if I were being tailed, there was nothing I could do about it. And the way things looked now, my days as a free man were numbered.

"Maybe it was a dumb idea to have people run around looking for blackmail material," I said to Gabrielle while I warmed up leftover pot roast for us. Thankfully, no one followed us home—at least as far as I knew. "But besides having my contacts dig up dirt, leaving Ms. Mendoza in charge of my case, keeping my mouth shut around government agents, and praying, I don't know what else to do." Gabrielle purred and rubbed against my legs. When I dished up her serving in her food bowl, she chowed down like she hadn't eaten in a week even though she'd been eating most of the day. Snarling at IIC agents, attacking fashion dolls, and crawling all over my office furniture must have worked up an appetite.

During dinner, I kept expecting government agents to ring my doorbell with an arrest warrant, but nothing happened. Actually, nothing like that happened for the next eight days. Proper sleep eluded me, but work at Trevalu Intergalactic Spice Company felt bizarrely normal. I tried my best not to knock on Ms. Mendoza's door every hour for updates, but it was hard not to micromanage with my freedom on the line. Mom and Dad called to say that they were grounded at the conference site for at least another week due to severe geomagnetic storm warnings, for which I was secretly grateful. I appreciated their support, but there was enough drama around here without them adding to the theatrics.

About two weeks after that incriminating tabloid hit the digital newsstands, just when I stopped jumping at every creak, crack, pop, and bump at headquarters, I received a second visit from Burke and Givordox. Gabrielle sat on my desk with her back arched, ready for Round 2.

"Mr. Trevalu," Burke said, "we have a warrant to search all of Trevalu Intergalactic Spice Company, including your office and all incoming and outgoing communications."

They probably weren't going to find anything in my office or the company as a whole, but the fact they had a warrant for communications worried me. Just because I deleted the record of my conversations with Coaxie and Logan didn't mean the Interstellar Investigation Commission couldn't dig up residual data.

"Let me see your warrant, please," I said, trying to sound cooly detached. Inside, my mind screamed, *God, help me!*

Givordox put his portable holographic plate on my desk. The warrant hovered above it. As far as I knew, it was legitimate.

"I do not consent to any searches," I said, choosing my words carefully in accordance with Mendoza's instructions, "but I will not stop you."

Burke tightened his lip, but the emotion behind the twitch was unreadable. Then, he and Givordox proceeded to search through all my files and scan my furniture as though I was hiding something inside the fabric. When they inspected Gabrielle's bed and blanket, she chattered fiercely. Before I could stop her, she launched herself at Burke, shrieking, flapping her wings in his face, and pulling on his hair. Burke lost his balance and fell backwards. Gabrielle's bed flew across the room. Her blanket flung into Givordox's squishy face, sticking to it.

"Givvy, get it off! Get it off!" Burke shielded his face from Gabrielle's frantic flapping.

Givvy? I didn't have time to think about how strangely humorous it was to hear an IIC agent lose his cool and refer to his colleague by a nickname in the middle of an investigation.

"Gabrielle, stop!" I snapped my fingers. "Bad girl! Shoulder!"

Gabrielle grumbled, kicked Burke in the face with her hind foot, and then perched on my shoulder. Givordox continued to wrestle with the wool baby blanket adhering to his gelatinous face.

"I am so sorry, sir," I said, helping Burke up. I didn't want him to be hurt—okay, maybe a tiny, unchristian part of me wanted him to be mildly hurt for all the sleepless nights he caused me over the course of two weeks—but I was more concerned about Gabrielle getting shot or confiscated if I didn't act sufficiently contrite.

Burke shoved me aside and peeled the blanket away from Givordox's face, leaving behind some lint. A thin layer of Givordox's face stuck to the blanket, but he didn't seem pained by it. Givordox looked Burke over, presumably checking him for injuries, and Burke did the same to his partner. Hopefully, Givordox could regenerate the torn portion of his face. Some aliens with wobbly, springy exteriors could do that.

"Do you have a license for that wretched little beast?" Burke said, adjusting his collar. I just then noticed that Gabrielle's screeching, wing-flapping, scratch attack also caused some damage to his clothes. That shouldn't have surprised me considering she once tore up approximately two hundred sequined costumes belonging to the Marvelous Min Pins. But that was a story to share on a day when I didn't fear imminent arrest.

"Certainly, I have a license," I said. Gabrielle gripped my shoulders, tense.

"Prove it." Based on the visible chest movements beneath his torn, rumpled suit, Burke was on the verge of hyperventilating. His hair looked like he just rolled out of bed. It was too soon to tell for sure, but it looked like a bruise was forming under his eye where Gabrielle kicked him.

"With all respect, sir," I said, "unless you have a warrant specifically written for that purpose or have authorization from animal control, I don't need to prove that to you." It's not as though I couldn't prove my lawful ownership of Gabrielle, but I didn't want to let either of the agents near my watch lest they find evidence of my contact with Logan.

"Oh, I can't wait to put you on the next prison transport spaceship to Port Songroi. And I'm adding a charge of assault on a law enforcement officer with a dangerous animal as soon as I finish my work here. In the meantime, keep that little flying fuzzball under control or I'll secure a warrant for *its* arrest." Burke returned his attention to Gabrielle's bed and blanket, as though they concealed contraband. I held Gabrielle, trying to calm her.

"Come on, girl. Behave yourself."

She growled at the agents but didn't try to escape my grasp.

While the agents continued treating my office like a crime scene, something thumped in the hallway in regular intervals, like heavy footfalls.

"Did you call security on us?" Givordox said, realizing that the sounds belonged to Flubby before I did.

"No, I didn't." Great. All I needed was an extra charge for obstruction of justice, which Burke would surely write up even though I didn't call anybody.

Seconds later, Flubby appeared with Coaxie under tucked one arm like a rag doll.

"Mr. Trevalu," Flubby said, "I caught an intruder who claims you agreed to some sort of photography venture?"

Despite being carried with her arms and feet dangling several feet off of the floor, Coaxie grinned. "Greetings, Neanderthals," she said with a salute. "Hey, Henry."

"Uh, hi, Coaxie. Mr. Flubby, please put Ms. Royer down."

Flubby set her on the ground.

"Thanks for the ride, mister," Coaxie said, adjusting her camera strap.

"Um, thank you, Mr. Flubby." I wasn't sure if I should be glad Coaxie was here or not. "You may go now."

Flubby hesitated but then nodded and left. Coaxie put her hands on her hips. "And to think I almost outran that big lummox. Made it past the elevator though. After all, I wouldn't want to miss our scheduled photo op." She winked. Remembering our code signal/euphemism, I felt elated. *Thank you, God, that Coaxie Royer found some information.*

"Ms. Royer, was it?" Burke said, shining some sort of detector flashlight along the room's baseboards. "I'm afraid that we're in the middle of an investigation and-"

"Well, what a coinkydink. Turns out, that's exactly what I've been doing, but about you and your buddy, Givordox." She whipped out a portable holographic plate and placed it on my desk. While it booted up, she said, "By the way, Burke, how's Mrs. Burke doing?"

"Ma'am, I'm going to have to ask you to leave the premises." I'm not sure what Burke expected to find in the floor vent, but he poked around there anyway, armed with his fancy flashlight.

"Actually, Agent Burke," I said, "this is still my office, Ms. Royer is my guest, and I think you'll be very interested in what she has to say." *Please God, I pray she discovered something juicy that we can use to protect Logan and me!*

"Thanks, Henry." The holographic plate flashed a picture of the Pleasure Port, that bar in Port Songroi where Logan's former life was exposed in the tabloids. "It turns out that Logan Voyle isn't the only eager guest of the Pleasure Port." Coaxie flipped through the virtual pictures like a slideshow. "I looked through my old collection, and wouldn't you know that Burkie here is quite the dancer? Here he is with some scantily clad alien chick. Were you searching for evidence under her skirt, or something?"

Burke stood abruptly. If Coaxie saw the flaming murder in his eyes, she didn't care. Givordox looked at Burke askance, as though barely concealing his disgust with his partner's lewd behavior abroad. Either that, or he was steaming because Burke's actions could make the Interstellar Investigation Commission look bad. Plus, the poor guy was missing a tiny portion of his face, so that was reason enough to sport a less than placid expression.

"Admittedly, this isn't one of my better pics," Coaxie said, flipping through the hovering photos with her fingertips, "but here you are with some other alien chick. And another one. And another one. Oops. Actually, I think that one's a guy on closer inspection."

Something made a grinding noise. At first, I thought it came from some construction equipment outside, but then I noticed Givordox's throat pulsating. He stared at Burke. *Oh, Lord, please don't let Givordox be suffering an allergic reaction from the wool baby blanket that got plastered to his face.*

"Ms. Royer, blackmail is only effective if the intended victim is willing to pay for the blackmailer's silence." There was no emotion in Burke's voice, and it scared me. A good, old-fashioned honeytrap clearly wasn't going to do the trick. Or, in the case of Coaxie's photos, several honeytraps.

"There is nothing illegal in those photographs, and I am perfectly willing to face Mrs. Burke's… disapproval."

Well, so much for that then, I thought. *Either he's bluffing, or he really is shameless enough to come clean to his wife in order to convict Logan and me.*

To my surprise, Coaxie smirked. "Oh, I thought you might say that. That's why some little birdies and I have been keeping an eye on you two for more than a week. Try this one on for size." She flipped to a picture of Burke and Givordox checking into a run-down motel.

"Are you quite finished, Ms. Royer?" Burke said. "There's hardly anything salacious about two IIC agents renting a room near their current assignment."

I would have thought Burke was correct, except that Givordox's normally pale green skin looked almost white.

"Ah, but wait," Coaxie said, barely holding back a smile, "there's more."

She pushed a button on the holographic plate, and a gravelly voice clearly belonging to Givordox emerged from the speaker: "I'm gonna melt you like an Alodeon whore."

"Yeah, melt me, you magnificent stud." No question, that was Burke.

I covered my ears, afraid that hearing any more of this motel audio sex tape was crossing the line into mortal sin. Plus, who in their right mind wanted to hear two government agents' awful dirty talk? Gabrielle grabbed my hands, probably thinking I was playing a game.

Coaxie shut off the recording, so I felt safe enough to unplug my ears. "Well, boys, I don't suppose I have to tell you that Givordox is liable to be executed if that tape ever makes it to the press. Morality laws on his home world, Alodeo, are pretty strict. Sure, they'll forgive discreet flings between Alodeons, but cross-species relationships are a big, fat no-no. We're talking death by drowning plus shunning for the family. And Alodeon bounty hunters would have no qualms dragging old Givvy back home to face charges. Yeah, there's some other audio footage I didn't share with you guys where you call each other Givvy and Burkie. Seriously, yuck!"

Givordox's face visibly drooped like it was melting. Burke's eye twitched, and then he lunged for the holographic plate. Coaxie affected a yawn.

"Throw it out the window, if you like," she said. "I have plenty of copies."

Burke held the holographic plate in his tightly curled fist, but then loosened his grip to put it into his pocket.

"Keeping a memento of your big night, huh?" Coaxie said. "By the way, you guys really suck at being government agents. I mean, the fact that freelance photographers like me can get all that intel on supposedly trained people like you… Well, you suck. Plus, Burke, you're honestly a bit of a nympho." Her watch phone rang. "Perfect timing." She answered it. "Hey, Logan."

Logan's face hovered above her watch. "Hey, Coaxie. How's the blackmail operation going?" He looked around. "Ah, based on Tweedledee and Tweedledum's expressions, I'd say it's going exceptionally well. Oh, hi, Henry."

"Hi, Logan," I said, still trying to process the scene in my mind. Two government agents caught in an intergalactic sex scandal with each other stood fuming in my office; the woman who exposed them stood calmly on the other side of my desk; Gabrielle nuzzled my cheek from her perch on my shoulder; and Logan's carefree image hovered above muckraker Coaxie Royer's watch phone.

"Hey, Burkie and Givvy," Logan said. "I had a lot of fun listening to those tapes Coaxie sent. I'm sorry it didn't include video because I'm honestly curious about the mechanics of human-Alodeon lovemaking. Anyway, before you two pop a gasket, get a load of this: I did a little investigating of my own this past week among my fellow ladies and gentlemen of the evening, and it turns out that your boss, Harlan Cain, has some sweetheart deal with Stellacross Enterprises. I don't know what kind of dirt the CEO of Stellacross Enterprises has on the head of the Interstellar Investigation Commission, but he has it set up so that any cargo ships owned by Stellacross Enterprises don't have to declare that they have comfort officers aboard, a clear legal violation in some galactic sectors that's considered akin to sex trafficking. A few more days of digging, and my buddies and I might figure out why this exception has been made. Unless, of course, you'd like to drop all of the charges against Henry Trevalu and me with full pardon and amnesty."

Burke and Givordox looked at each other and then redirected their attention to the rest of us. An uncomfortable silence followed—well, uncomfortable for the two agents, anyway.

Mendoza knocked on the outside of my open office door, holding her laptop under one arm.

"Come in, Ms. Mendoza," I said, silently thanking God for what I sensed was yet another example of perfect timing.

"Mr. Trevalu, Agents, um… Are you with the press?" She eyed Coaxie's camera equipment.

"Coaxie Royer, freelance photographer at the highest bidder's service," she said with an exaggerated stage bow.

"Oh, how do you do, Ms. Royer?"

"Pretty good after making these space cadets eat a full serving of humble pie."

The agents said nothing about the offhanded insult, only swallowed.

"By the way, I've got Logan on the phone." Coaxie held up her wrist to show Logan's image.

"Ah, Mr. Voyle," Mendoza said. "I didn't expect to see you here."

"Well, hey there, Ms. Mendoza. It's turning into one big company picnic around here."

"I quite agree, Mr. Voyle. And since you're all here, this is the perfect time to explain my findings on this case as it pertains to all of you, and that includes the media. With your permission, Mr. Trevalu?"

"Gladly," I said. Gabrielle chirped in agreement.

Mendoza set her laptop on my desk and popped it open. "It took me most of the week, but I have discovered two clauses that can make Logan Voyle's contract with the Interstellar One merchant spaceship, *Soaring Raptor*, null and void." She pulled up the contract. "First, Logan Voyle signed onto the ship under the false identity, Piper Long. This fraud, while possibly punishable by a fine, means that Logan Voyle never legally agreed to the terms of his contract. Were this discovered during his time aboard the *Soaring Raptor*, he likely would have been dishonorably discharged. Second, there is a little-known provision in the contract for termination by buyout. I needed to research this for a few days because the law is old, obscure, and rarely called upon. In short, Mr. Trevalu, you could purchase Mr. Voyle's contract and allow him to serve on one of your ships for the remainder of his term. Of course, since Trevalu Intergalactic Spice Company doesn't hire comfort officers as a matter of principle, you could simply have Mr. Voyle serve on one of your cargo ships in a non-sexual capacity."

"Thank you, Ms. Mendoza," I said. For the first time in nearly two weeks, my chest felt like it was expanding and contracting properly. "What do you say, Agent Burke and Agent Givordox? Why don't we save ourselves a huge legal mess and forget that all these scandals ever happened?"

Burke and Givordox looked at each other, and then back at us.

"In light of Ms. Mendoza's legal findings," Burke said, clearing his throat, "the Interstellar Investigation Commission will drop all charges against Logan Voyle and Henry Trevalu and grant full pardon and amnesty for all related crimes. This is provided, of course, that Ms. Royer's compromising photographs, audio, and any existing video clips not be leaked to the public. I would demand that they be destroyed, but I know that you're too intelligent to leave yourself without insurance."

"Ya got that right, Burkie," Coaxie said, beaming.

"Also," Burke said, glowering at her, "don't call me that."

"Okay, okay. One playthrough of the audio was more than enough for me anyhow. Seriously, the word 'melt' isn't sexy. Well, I've outstayed my welcome, as usual. See ya!"

Coaxie hustled out of my office before Logan had a chance to make any parting remarks from her watch phone. Ms. Mendoza excused herself to draw up some legal documents, leaving me and Gabrielle with the agents.

"You're terribly cruel for a man of faith." The sadness in Givordox's voice surprised me.

"*I'm* terribly cruel?" I said, trying not to raise my voice. Gabrielle jumped onto my desk, keeping her eyes fixed on the two men who disturbed her bed earlier. "You literally chase down runaway ship's prostitutes for a living, forcing them to serve out the remainder of their evil contracts."

"We're only enforcing legally binding contracts signed by consenting adults," Burke said. "That's hardly cruelty when the comfort officers signed up for it."

"Consenting adults? Sorry, but you don't know a steaming pile of crap about those supposedly consenting adults. People don't sign up to be comfort officers because they have good educations and great job prospects. Once they realize what a degrading meat grinder the job really is, some of them understandably flee. And that's when people like you come in to hunt them down along with those who help them escape. Don't talk to me about cruelty when you're basically enforcing legal, institutionalized rape."

I sat down at my desk and scribbled something on a piece of paper, trying to make myself look busy so these disgusting creeps would leave my office once and for all. For my part, I had no guilt about my alleged cruelty. As the good Lord said, settle out of court, be cunning as serpents, and be harmless as doves. Other than Gabrielle's outburst, no one got hurt— at least not badly—so no harm done. On top of all that, Logan would be safe to return to Trevalu Intergalactic Spice Company to resume his position as the supply chain ethics manager—possibly aboard a spaceship to be in compliance with his comfort officer contract's buyout clause. And I wouldn't do any time in Port Songroi Jail. If that didn't constitute a win-win for everyone, what did? *Thank you, Jesus, that everything worked out. Amen.*

"And yet, you orchestrated this counter-investigation that could have led to my execution and my family's shunning for life."

Givordox's words made me stop doodling and look at him.

"I had no idea that anything Coaxie dug up might endanger you or your family," I said, feeling an annoying prickle in my conscience. Although it wasn't prickly enough to make me one hundred percent sympathetic to his plight. "But with all respect, you and Agent Burke were determined to send Logan back to the *Soaring Raptor* and me to Port Songroi Jail. Both of us would have been seriously harmed. I don't like to play dirty with blackmail and such, but I was trying to stop harm, not cause it."

Burke ran his hand through his hair, which was still mussed up from Gabrielle's attack. He also had an unmistakable purple bruise under his eye. "Look, Mr. Trevalu, we're only doing our jobs."

"Agent Burke, most of the galaxy's tyranny has been perpetuated with that sadly craven statement, 'we're only doing our jobs.'" Gabrielle cocked her head and stared at me wide-eyed, surprised as I was at my calm, unexpected eloquence. I stood, feeling oddly tranquil.

"You can both quit, you know. It's not like you have to be Interstellar Investigation Commission agents anymore."

"You have us all wrong, Mr. Trevalu," Burke said. "You make it sound as though all we do is chase fugitive prostitutes. The Interstellar Investigation Commission does a lot of good in the galaxy. We pursue sex traffickers, drug traffickers, arms traffickers, poachers, art thieves, kidnappers, murderers… Look, I shouldn't have to list our entire résumé to convince you that we aren't some vile entity trying to swallow every planet in our path with evil and destruction."

I sighed. "The good you might do in the galaxy doesn't cancel out the bad. But I'm not going to argue with you, Agent Burke. And I'll pray that you and Mrs. Burke can work things out. Now, please, will you and Agent Givordox see yourselves out, or should Mr. Flubby guide you to the exit?"

"All right," Burke said. "We're leaving, you treacherous little snake." After he and Givordox left the room, Burke popped his head back into my office and said, "By the way, you can tell your disgusting little friend, Coaxie Royer, that 'melt' happens to be the sexiest word in the Alodeon language." That time, he left and didn't come back. *Good riddance.*

Relieved that Mendoza, Logan, Coaxie, and I defeated the IIC, I petted Gabrielle and prayed a Rosary of gratitude. Seconds after I said my last *Amen*, my watch dinged with an alert. Coaxie and her "undercover crew" sent me an invoice for 500,000 universal credits. The note on the invoice read, "for photographic and audio services rendered."

Right, I thought as I pulled up one of my bank accounts, *justice doesn't come cheap. But it's well worth it to keep Logan and me out of the slammer.* By the end of the week, I would probably get a big, fat bill from Mendoza too. She may have been on retainer, but that didn't mean everything was included. *Thank you, God, that I'm loaded.*

Rapid footsteps echoed in the hall. Before I could figure out what interruption would disturb my day next, Mom and Dad burst into my office, hugged me, and started asking a multitude of questions at once: *How are you? Did Ms. Mendoza straighten things out? Is Logan safe? Is the investigation still ongoing? We heard rumors that the case was closed. Is that true?* And on and on and on. Gabrielle trilled like an old-fashioned telephone while flying around them in a circle, ecstatic to see them for the first time in over two weeks. It was the only awesome form of chaos I'd experienced since my parents' departure for their conference.

"Yes, yes, I'm fine," I said. "And Logan's safe." Gabrielle jumped on Dad's shoulder, seeking attention. She chattered close to his ear as though giving her account of the recent events in her own words. "Like I said before, Ms. Mendoza is on the job. Thanks to a couple of loopholes she discovered in Logan's contract, the case is as good as closed. Plus, the agents dropped all charges against me in light of all the findings."

"Oh, thanks be to God," Mom said, hugging me again. "I can't face another prison sentence in the family that winds up with you giving birth to two thousand precocial Uhumbra on an alien world."

I didn't bother explaining for the umpteenth time that being a somewhat unwilling surrogate to alien pseudo-octopus fry was probably a one-time thing. *Thank God for that!* Besides, I wouldn't have been able to get a word in anyway. Mom and Dad resumed bombarding me with questions, firing them out faster than I could possibly answer them. When there was finally a lull, I simply said, "Don't worry. We settled the whole thing out of court, just like the good Lord taught."

The End

ABOUT THE AUTHOR

E.J. LeRoy is a freelance writer whose work has appeared in several speculative fiction publications including *After the Storm Magazine*, *Androids and Dragons*, and *NonBinary Review*. Henry Trevalu is a recurring character whose intergalactic misadventures are cataloged on the author's website here:

https://ejleroy.weebly.com/series.html.

Thank you for reading this special issue!

*For more great reads check out quarterly issues
of Adventures Bookzine at:
ReadAdventures.com*